CHAPTER 1
Ginny

Ginny rushed down the lighthouse stairs and into the large dining room that also served as her restaurant, The Lighthouse Café. She clutched the small leather-bound book in her hand as she greeted her daughters, Reece and Chandler, as well as Chandler's boyfriend, Hudson.

The sun was sinking down the horizon, splashing tangerine and wheat colors across the floor. Her girls and Hudson sat in front of an impressive spread of food that Reece had made for them.

"Come and sit," Reece said. "I've got some special dishes that I'd like for y'all to taste."

"It smells like heaven," Chandler told her.

One side of Reece's mouth tipped into a smile. It warmed Ginny's heart to see her daughters bonding over food. Only recently, those two had been at each other's throats. Of course, that had occurred at the same time as Ginny's secret had come out—that her husband and their father, Jack, had kept a mistress and had willed their home to that mistress upon his death.

Hence how Ginny had found herself buying a lighthouse and turning the place into a restaurant.

"What do we have here?" Ginny said, slipping onto a cane-backed chair.

"A feast," Hudson replied with a twinkle in his eyes.

He was the perfect complement to her daughter, who had creamy skin and platinum-blonde hair. Hudson was blessed with brown hair and eyes, plus a kind demeanor and steady, calm presence.

Reece splayed her hands on the table and grinned proudly. "We've got shrimp and grits, tomato salad drizzled with balsamic dressing and topped with goat cheese, and peach cobbler for dessert."

"You're trying to make me fat," Ginny joked.

"Not at all," her daughter replied, shaking her head. "But we might as well try out new recipes and see what we like. How else will we know what to serve in the café?"

She said it in a very businesslike voice, but it was obvious that Reece really just wanted an excuse to eat shrimp and experiment with a new dessert.

The shrimp had been grilled, and the shells were browned. They sat atop a bed of steaming grits with a buttery sauce spooned on top. Flat cilantro leaves garnished the dish, and it looked divine.

The tomato salad was a splash of color with golden- and plum-hued heirloom tomatoes sliced and drizzled with olive oil, dressing and creamy feta.

The peach cobbler, the last and probably the best looking of all the meal, sat in a robin's-egg-blue casserole dish. A browned crumbly crust covered bubbling peaches that were thickened with sugar.

Her stomach grumbled, which elicited a laugh from Chandler. "Hungry, Mama?"

"Starving."

Reece passed the bowl of shrimp, and Ginny scooped some onto her plate. The smell was even more delectable than the appearance. The fresh Gulf shrimp reminded her of the ocean at their backs, and the grits reminded her of the Southern roots that she shared with her daughters.

"What's that book?" Reece asked as she draped a napkin in her lap.

"Oh, I was so overcome with the food that I almost forgot all about it."

Chandler elbowed her sister playfully. "Look who's becoming quite the chef."

The Lighthouse Secret

GULF COAST GETAWAY BOOK 2

BEBE REED

"I'm not that good," she murmured, but red tinged the cheeks of Ginny's youngest. She cleared her throat, clearly embarrassed, and nodded to the journal. "What is that? Are you trying to avoid my question?"

Ginny laughed and swiped a napkin over her mouth. "Not at all. I was up in the tower, and I spotted it peeking out from one of the slats. But you'll never believe what it is."

"Now *I'm* curious," Hudson added.

Ginny traced her finger over the gilded border that wrapped around the brown cover. The leather was cracked and peeling in some areas, but for as old as she assumed it was, easily over sixty years, it was still in good condition.

"It looks to be Emma Grace's diary."

Reece's mouth dropped. "Not *the* Emma Grace."

"The very same."

Chandler's gaze darted to Ginny. "You're talking about the lighthouse keeper's daughter."

"The one and the same." She couldn't keep the smile off her face. "How many other Emma Graces could there be?"

"Now you have me even more curious." Hudson draped a hand over the back of Chandler's chair. "Who's Emma Grace?"

Reece barreled into the story before anyone else. Typical Reece, she was all fireball and courage, very different from Chandler, who was more reserved, thoughtful.

Reece's hands flicked up and down excitedly as she spoke. "A long time ago, at least from what we've been told, Emma Grace lived here, in the lighthouse. She was in love with a fisherman's son, but the fisherman and her father despised one another."

Hudson's brow quirked. "And the drama starts already."

"But that's the thing," she told him. "We don't know how much or how deep their actual hatred ran. All we know is that they didn't like one another, creating a total Romeo-and-Juliet situation between Emma Grace and what's his name."

At Hudson's puzzled look, Chandler said, "We don't actually know his name."

"I see."

3

"So," Reece continued, "apparently the two were kept apart, pining for one another"—at that Ginny laughed—"until one night a terrible storm hit the Gulf. While Emma and her father were changing the light, the fisherman's boat crashed along the rocks. When they got the light back on, Emma realized what had happened. She rushed out of the lighthouse and was never seen again."

"That's what we've heard," Ginny clarified to Hudson. "Folklore and truth can often be very different from one another."

"I prefer to think of them as star-crossed lovers." Reece slapped a hand against her chest. "Emma Grace didn't want to face a world without the love of her life, so she ended it all, throwing herself into the ocean to be with him."

Chandler picked at her salad. "Rather morbid, don't you think?"

"Romantic," she replied with a dramatic sigh.

"Whichever it was, the answers are in here." Ginny tapped the book. "Maybe not all of them, but certainly some. So, who's going to read it?"

She expected Reece to throw up her hand, but that didn't happen. Chandler pressed her lips together in an attempt to hide a smile while Hudson shrugged.

"You," her youngest said. "You're going to read it."

Ginny barked a laugh. "Me? Why me?"

"Because you found it. Why else?"

"Well, because..." Because she was too busy? Because she didn't believe in love anymore? Because she wasn't curious about what had happened to Emma Grace?

None of those things were true. Even after what Jack had done to her, she still believed in love. She wasn't *in love* with anyone, but she liked Aiden, a local treasure hunter who was slowly working his way into her life. As soon as Aiden's face popped into her mind—salt-and-pepper hair, tanned skin, sparkling blue eyes—she forced it out. There were plenty of other things to think about than him.

But the butterflies circling in her stomach suggested that she liked thinking about him more than she wanted to admit.

She sighed and dropped her gaze to the diary. Honestly there wasn't any reason *not* to read it. She had the time, and if she was being honest with herself, curiosity pinged inside her at the thought of finding out what led up to the events before the storm.

"Okay, I'll read it."

"Good, and you can tell us all about it," Chandler said. "Which reminds me."

"Of what?" Reece asked, then popped a shrimp into her mouth.

She folded one corner of her napkin in a distracted manner. "Hudson and I have something we'd like to tell y'all."

Ginny perked up. Hudson had only just moved to Sugar Cove after relocating from New York City to be with Chandler. Her heart tightened. Had Hudson asked her to move in with him? She loved having her oldest daughter with her in the lighthouse, but at the same time she knew that Chandler would have to get on with her life and leave the nest...again.

"Y-yes? What is it?"

"Well"—Chandler's gaze slid to Hudson, who nodded reassuringly—"Hudson proposed and I said yes!"

"Oh, darlin'!" Ginny rose and flung out her arms to hug her daughter. "That's wonderful news."

"Are you happy for us, Mama?"

"So happy." Hudson stood by himself, and she gestured for him to enter the hug. He did, and they squeezed into a circle for a moment before the trio each took a step back. She knuckled tears from her eyes. "This is the best news that I ever could've heard."

Chandler winked. "Better than the journal?"

"So much better."

"I apologize for not asking your permission first," he told her.

"That's all right. It's customary to ask the father's permission, and he's not here." She patted his shoulder. "But if it makes you feel any better, I'm sure Jack would've given his blessing."

"Yeah, he's probably looking down on us right now and smiling," Reece blurted out.

The three women exchanged a look. Reece had meant well, but uneasiness blanketed the room. Surely Jack wasn't looking down on them, not after his transgressions. More than likely, he was staring up from the other place, but Ginny kept her mouth shut.

Her youngest seemed to sense that she'd misspoken, so she quickly added, "Where's the ring?"

Chandler pulled it from her pocket and slipped it onto her finger. "We wanted to surprise you and not start off dinner with the announcement."

"Why not? I love good news. Let's sit." They sat and Ginny scooped peach cobbler onto dessert plates. "Now we have an extra reason to enjoy this cobbler."

Chandler bit into the gooey peaches topped with a hard crust and moaned. "I'm going to need you to become my personal chef, Reece."

She barked a laugh. "How about I teach you how to cook this well?"

"I'd rather stick to jewelry design."

"How's that going?" Ginny asked.

Hudson smiled at Chandler. "She's got good news about that, too."

Her oldest settled her fork atop her plate. "Vicki called me today and said that I can have space in her store to sell my own work."

"That's so cool," Reece announced. "Double congrats!"

"Thank you."

She hated to be pushy, but as a mother there were certain things she wanted to know. "Have you thought about a date yet? For the wedding?"

"Mama, we only just got engaged," Chandler scolded lightly.

"I know, but it's never too early to figure it out."

"We discussed it a little, Mrs. Rigby."

"Please Hudson, call me Ginny."

Not only because they were going to be related, but also because she couldn't stand being associated with Jack. Not anymore.

He cleared his throat. "Chandler and I"—he took her hand—"talked about having the wedding in the spring."

"That would be a beautiful time to have it. If you have the wedding here, it won't be too hot, or even if you had it up north, closer to Hudson's family, springtime would be beautiful."

Hudson smiled at Chandler. "Our lives are here now. I don't want to speak for my fiancée"—he kissed the back of her hand—"but I think that having the wedding in Sugar Cove would be special. It would also introduce my family to my new life."

"And how's that going?" she asked, referring to the fact that Hudson had just bought a house on the beach and would be starting at his law firm's coastal office soon.

"Great so far. Soon as I'm all settled in, I'll report for duty."

Reece chuckled. "You make it sound like you're entering the army."

"The law takes up a lot of time."

"But hopefully the beach will counter some of the stress," Chandler said pointedly.

"I can just see you, Hudson, wearing Hawaiian shirts and cargo shorts to work," Reece joked.

He laughed at that. "Things may be more relaxed here, but they're not *that* relaxed."

Laughter sparked from everyone at the table. Ginny smiled, her heart full as she took in the happy couple across from her.

She wished to be that happy again and have a man in her life. But for now she'd settle on living vicariously through Emma Grace and her journal. She wondered what secrets would be revealed in the brittle pages of the diary.

CHAPTER 2
Ginny

But Ginny did not crack open the diary that evening. Instead she slipped it onto her nightstand and gave it a good long look before switching off the lamp and going to sleep.

She put it out of her head all the next morning, too, until she strolled into the kitchen and strapped on her apron.

Reece was already hard at work as she stacked fried pies onto a tray and slid them into the display case that kept them cool.

"So," her daughter said as she dusted flour from her hands, "when will you be hiring someone new?"

She pulled her hair back and tied it. "What do you mean?"

"Come on, Mama. Chandler isn't going to stay forever, especially not since she's engaged."

Her stomach dropped. She'd been so busy being happy for her oldest that she hadn't bothered considering what it actually meant for the café.

"She's been working more on her jewelry, too," Reece added, which seemed to make the hole that had opened in Ginny's stomach bigger. "This isn't her thing. I wish it was, but she's not big into cooking."

Her daughter was right. The café might've been Ginny's dream, but it wasn't Chandler's. Reece loved baking and cooking, so the café offered that outlet for her. But for her eldest, this wasn't the end all be all.

"I'll figure it out."

Reece slid by carrying a stack of white porcelain plates. "Did you read any of the diary?"

"Um, no. I was so tired last night."

"Why not? If you don't want to read it, I will. Who doesn't want to read a tragic love story?"

She, for one, didn't. Having lived out her own tragic love story had given her enough hurt to last a lifetime.

But she couldn't look so weak to her children.

"I'll get to it," she promised.

"You'd better," Reece added with a wink.

"What had Mama better do?" Chandler asked, sailing in, her face scrubbed pink and her wheat-colored hair pulled away from her face.

Ginny shot Reece a look. "Nothing for you to worry about. Come on. Let's get ready for the first lunch service."

* * *

By the time the doors opened for lunch, a line of people wound down the sidewalk and into the parking lot.

"What's on the menu today?" several people asked as they slipped into the cool dining room.

"Crab quiche. It's delicate enough for the ladies, but hearty enough for you strapping men," she told one man who wore an orange construction vest.

"I'm sure it'll be great," he replied as she led him to an empty table.

Ginny had just sat the last guest when an old woman, probably in her eighties or maybe even nineties, walked toward the café, her arm hooked around a man's elbow. She used a cane to steady herself, and she wore the brightest colors—a gauzy teal scarf was wrapped around her throat, and a coral hat topped her head.

Her escort, by comparison, was not only at least fifty years younger, but he was also dressed in opposite colors, wearing a black suit with a thin ebony tie. Wearing such heavy clothing to the beach made Ginny break into a sweat. He led the woman to the door and opened it for her.

Oh no. There weren't any tables left, and there hadn't been time to place the placard outside that read *Lunch Service Full, Please Come Again*.

Perhaps she could offer the couple a to-go container of lunch.

"Welcome to the Lighthouse Café," she said, donning her brightest smile. "I'm afraid this lunch service is full."

The woman's weepy gaze swept around the room. She had a cold, reserved look about her and didn't seem to notice Ginny until her escort nudged her. "Mrs. Travis."

The woman's eyes narrowed. "Are you the owner of this establishment?"

Ginny hadn't felt so judged in...well, since Jack had been alive. She nearly withered. "Yes, I am. My name's Ginny Rigby."

"And you've turned this lighthouse into a café?"

"Yes, ma'am. That's correct." She pointed to the framed article on the wall that the critic Reynold Thompkins had published only a few short weeks ago. "We've been blessed to have been successful."

"I've heard," Mrs. Travis snipped. "That's why I'm here."

"I'm afraid that this lunch service is full," she explained. The confused expression on the old woman's face told Ginny that an explanation was needed. "You see, every day we cook one meal that has a starter, a main course and dessert. We serve one menu because there are only three of us who work here—me and my daughters. We have two lunch services, and this one is full. The next is in an hour, if you'd like to come back, or I can make y'all plates to go. Whatever you'd prefer."

"I haven't come for lunch," she replied, lifting her nose.

"Oh?"

Mrs. Travis unhooked her arm from the escort and placed both knotted hands on her cane. "I'm part of the Teal Scarf Society."

"I'm not familiar."

"We are a charitable organization of women who wear teal scarves to signify that we're part of the group. Our causes champion women and children. This year we're meeting here, in Sugar Cove."

And what did that have to do with Ginny? She did her best to keep her face blank. "How wonderful. I'm sure it's rewarding work."

The woman's gaze sharpened as if to say, *You wouldn't know anything about it because you're not in it.* "Yes, it is. But the reason why I'm here is because I have heard of your restaurant, and I would like for your café to cater our event."

"You would?" Her heart soared. Booking events like this could pave the way for the café to start making a name for itself. "When is it?"

"Several weeks away. I'd like to discuss the details with you at another time. Today I only wanted to meet you."

"Certainly. Whatever you'd prefer."

"That's what I'd prefer," Mrs. Travis replied in a prickly voice. "My assistant will call you to set up the appointment. Sam, please get her number."

With that, Mrs. Travis turned away as if the conversation was done and she no longer had any use for her. Ginny, on the other hand, did her best not to let the old woman's demeanor ruffle her feathers. It wasn't often that you found an old Southern woman to be rude and curmudgeonly, but Mrs. Travis was all of that and probably much more.

The old woman's attitude made it tempting to turn down the offer to cater, but this could work in her favor, so Ginny gave Sam her phone number and the two made their way out the door just as someone was approaching.

She was poised to tell the customer that the lunch service was full until she got a good look at him—brown hair with flecks of salty gray above the ears, sparkling blue eyes, lean brown muscles.

Aiden held the door as Mrs. Travis and Sam exited. Ginny shook her head and strode up, watching as Sam led the old woman to a sleek black town car.

"What was that all about?" Aiden asked.

"How do you know it was about anything?" she teased.

"If the look on your face is any indication, it was about quite a lot."

"That is Mrs. Travis, and she wants us to cater an event for her. Ever heard of the Teal Scarf Society?"

He frowned, which made the corners of his eyes crinkle in the most delicious way. "Can't say that I have."

"That makes two of us."

Aiden smiled at her, and Ginny felt like she'd been sucked into a funnel of light, like all the happiness in the world was focused on her. The look in his eyes was so intense that it made her stomach quiver, a sensation she hadn't experienced in...well, in forever. Or so it seemed.

"Oh, you'll never believe what I found?"

"Is that a real question?" he teased. "Am I supposed to guess or are you just going to tell me."

She batted at him. "I'm going to tell you. But you'll have to wait until next service. I've got tables to bus and sweet tea to refill."

He scanned the dining room. "Doesn't look like there are any seats left."

She rolled her eyes. "You've always got a seat in the kitchen." That sounded pushy, didn't it? "That's if you want it. I don't mean to force anything on you."

He leaned forward and dropped his mouth to her ear. "Ginny Rigby, there's very little you could force on me."

Her stomach somersaulted and she couldn't help but to beam even as her cheeks flamed with heat. "Come on. Let me get you that seat."

She led Aiden through the dining room and to a small counter in the kitchen, where she served him a green salad and steaming crab quiche with a side of green beans that had simmered in a broth seasoned with bacon, plus garlic roasted potatoes.

"This is country cooking with a side of class," Aiden said proudly.

Ginny laughed. "It's a good description."

She smiled down at him, and he grinned. The urge to brush her hand over his shoulder wrestled inside of her, but she let it go. They were taking things slowly, and she wasn't in a place where jumping into a relationship sounded like a good idea. Her heart required more healing for that to happen.

But still, the hole in her heart was slowly healing, day by day, and just seeing Aiden seemed to mend it a bit more.

"I'll come back for your review later," she told him, smiling.

The next few minutes were busy as she refilled glasses, rang up customers (who all loved the crab and reveled at the fried pies that Reece had cooked up) and cleaned tables.

When the first lunch service was officially over, she returned to Aiden, who was slicing his fork into a pie.

"Did Reece tell you what kind she made?"

A twinkle filled his eyes. "Peach, she said. I can never turn down anything with peaches in it. Come and sit. You're welcome to a bite."

She waved off his offer of pie but did sit. "After I found your note in the tower, I found something else."

"Right. The story you were hinting that you're *dying* to tell me."

"I'm not dying," she countered playfully. "Though if anyone is dying to tell something, it's Chandler."

He swiped a napkin over his mouth. "Why's that?"

"Last night she got engaged."

"No kidding." He spotted her over Ginny's shoulder. "Best wishes, Chandler."

She wiggled her fingers to show off the ring. "Thank you."

"When's the wedding?"

"We're still figuring that out."

"There's time," he replied before turning back. "Now. You were saying."

"After I found your note, I discovered something else hidden in the tower, and it may surprise you as much as it did to me."

Aiden's arm paused in the air, leaving his fork suspended with a slice of gooey fried pie nestled atop it. "Well don't leave me in suspense."

"I found Emma Grace's diary."

His eyes widened. "Emma Grace as in *the Emma Grace* who lived in the lighthouse all those years ago?"

"Has to be."

"What does it say? Don't leave me in suspense."

"I haven't read it yet."

"What? You didn't stay up all night soaking in those pages?"

She shook her head.

"I sense a wall."

"There's no wall."

He shrugged. "Then there's no reason *not* to read it."

She sighed in frustration. "I'll get to it."

"What are you doing tomorrow?"

"It's Saturday; the restaurant's closed. I'm free."

"You're not anymore."

Ginny scoffed. "I'm not?"

"No." He took the last bite of his pie and rose, patting his stomach. "That was the best meal I've had since the last time I ate here."

She ducked her head in embarrassment. "You flatter me."

"Not at all." He pulled out his wallet and paid for the meal. "I'll pick you up at four. Be hungry."

"Now I'm intrigued."

"Good." He winked. "My goal is to make sure you stay that way."

CHAPTER 3
Chandler

Chandler Rigby was on cloud nine. She'd always felt that eventually she and Hudson would marry, but she'd never expected it to be so soon.

"How's the bracelet coming?"

Vicki Orr peeked into the studio. She owned the jewelry shop and had been kind enough to allow Chandler to use her equipment to create new works.

She lifted the strand of pearls linked together with a delicate silver chain. "What do you think?"

"Let me take a closer look." Vicki plucked her peacock-blue reading glasses from where they rested on a chain atop her chest and slid them onto her nose. She crossed the room and sucked in a breath. "It's one of the nicest pieces you've created so far. So delicate. You'll quickly find a buyer for it."

"Thank you," she replied, working a cloth over the pearls to clean them.

"You know," the store owner told her, "you're welcome to bring your own equipment here. There's plenty of room in the studio."

"I know, but Hudson has so much space in his house. We're setting up a room for all of it now. Plus I've intruded more than enough here, don't you think?"

She tsked. "I don't think you've intruded enough."

Chandler smiled. "You've been more than kind. Besides, I've had a new development in my life."

Her brown eyebrows lifted in intrigue. "Is that so?"

She lifted her left hand and displayed the engagement ring. "Hudson proposed."

"That's wonderful. I'm happy for you."

But there was something off about Vicki's smile. "I'm excited. I never expected this to happen so soon."

"He did move here for you."

"Yes, but I thought it would be another year before a proposal came."

"When you know it's right, then you know it's right."

Warmth spread across Chandler's stomach. "I think that's true."

Vicki took a step back and surveyed her. "Was it hard to say yes? Even though it felt right?"

She frowned, feeling a divot dimple between her eyebrows. "What do you mean?"

"Never mind." She waved her hand dismissively. "It's nothing."

But it didn't seem like nothing. Vicki had given her good solid life advice before, so curiosity won over when she said, "Even if it's nothing, I want to hear it."

The store owner nodded morosely. "It's just that I wonder if the past caused you to hesitate at all."

"Hesitate?"

"What with everything that happened with your father. I'd hate for that to have any bearing on your future, but from what you told me, since it was such a horrible betrayal, it seems like it has to play in the back of your mind."

Her words struck Chandler like a slap to the face. No, she hadn't thought much about what her father had done to her mother. Putting it out of her mind had been the best course of action for weeks. It didn't help Mama for him to come up in every conversation, so mostly the topic hadn't been discussed.

In fact, the entire betrayal was buried deep down in a place where it was locked away. There had *been* no correlation between Hudson's proposal and her father's actions, but now that was all she could think about.

As Vicki left the room, doubt whirled in Chandler's mind. Her father had kept a secret family from them. Hudson loved her, but she'd also thought that her father had loved her mother. He'd never doted, no, but all relationships were different.

Hudson was different than her father had been, she knew that. But then why was a seed of doubt sprouting in her heart, a seed that quietly whispered to her that the past would repeat itself, that she would wind up in a situation exactly like her mother's?

CHAPTER 4
Reece

"Are you ready?"

Reece stood atop the shaded porch wearing white shorts and a coral-colored top with a light sweater pulled over her shoulders.

Shelby, her best friend, exited the front door and called back, "I'll be back in a bit, Nana!"

"You girls have fun," Vera yelled. "Good to see you, Reece."

"Good to see you, Ms. Vera," she replied.

Shelby shut the front door of the beach cottage and ran her fingers through her thick, strawberry-blonde locks. Reece could've been jealous of her friend's beauty, but she adored her too much to let something as petty as jealousy get in the way.

"You ready to do some shopping?"

Reece flashed a smile. "So ready."

After a week of getting up at two in the morning to start baking for the day, she more than needed to blow off some steam.

"I thought you'd say that. Let's go have some fun."

They drove to Apalachicola with the windows down. The briny breeze lashed at her hair, messing it, but she didn't care. She loved the way the beach sun warmed her skin, how it ignited her passion for living. There was only one thing missing in her life.

"I saw Ted the other day," her bestie said casually.

She tried to sound uninterested when she asked, "How's he?"

"As gorgeous as ever."

Ted *was* gorgeous with sandy hair, broad shoulders and a jawline that went on forever. Her heart ached just thinking about him.

"But he didn't ask me out," Shelby said with a sigh. "I don't think he ever will. Ugh. Tell me the truth—am I pining for the wrong man?"

Her heart twisted. "I don't know. How could he not like you? You're beautiful."

"But he doesn't seem interested. Maybe there's someone else that he *is* interested in."

Reece pursed her lips. There *was* someone else that he was interested in—her. But she couldn't reveal that and hurt her best friend.

"He'll come around and ask you out. Just you wait."

She scoffed. "I'll probably be dead by then."

"Don't say that."

Shelby gave her the side-eye. "I don't know. Oh, look. We're here. Let's find a place to park."

Downtown Apalachicola was chock-full of small-town Southern charm. It was rare to find such a thing in Florida, but this part of the state, the Panhandle, which was closest to the deep Southern states, still held on to what made the South distinct from the rest of the country—hospitality, friendliness and a sense of welcome.

After parking the little sports car, the two got out, heading into Apalach Outfitters, a wonderful clothing and outdoor boutique.

"They should have the fall clothes in," Shelby said, glancing over her shoulder as she opened the door. "I can't wait to see what they've got."

She had just faced forward when she collided with a man exiting the store. He was a good head taller with short ebony hair, piercing eyes and muscled arms that refused to hide under his T-shirt.

And Shelby's face was plastered squarely in the middle of his chest.

"Oh, I'm so sorry," she yelped.

The man gently took her by the shoulders and pushed her back. "It's all righ— Shelby, is that you?"

"Batton Deats?"

He smiled then, his face beaming down. "Yeah, it's me."

Her voice hardened to ice. "What are you doing here?"

Batton immediately stiffened, his face becoming stone. "Just staying in town awhile."

"I thought that you were living up north."

"I was. I am. Like I said, it's just for a while."

The hairs on the back of Reece's neck soldiered to attention. Shelby's guard was up with this guy, even though he'd been happy to see her. But now *his* guard was up, too, and the air was thick with tension. So thick that it could've been cut like a hot knife running through butter. There was a story here, and she had to know what it was.

Shelby lifted her nose. "Well, anyway. Have a good one."

A shadow crossed Batton's face, and his eyes flashed with what looked like sorrow. "Sure thing. You too."

They moved to pass one another. Shelby moved to her right as he shifted to his left. Then she moved to the left and he shifted to his right.

He rubbed the back of his neck. "How about you go right, and I go right."

She huffed and moved as he suggested. Reece stayed out of the man's path as he exited.

By the time she caught up to Shelby, her friend was perusing a clothing rack, slamming blouses to the left with a raging vigor.

"What was that about?"

"What was *what* about?"

She rolled her eyes. "You're not serious. You and that Batton guy. Your anger was off the rails, and he was so nice at first. He was happy to see you."

"Oh, that."

"Yeah, that."

She was silent for a good long minute, and Reece shook her head in frustration. "As long as I've known you, which I will admit hasn't been too long, I've never seen you so angry at someone."

Her friend abandoned the rack she was searching through and headed toward another. Shelby wasn't going to get off that easily.

She followed her. "It just seems like there's history there, is all."

"How do you think this'll look?" She yanked a plum-colored crop top from the rack and pressed it to her stomach. "Should I try it on?"

"Of course you should. That color is perfect for you. But you're dodging the question."

"Fine." She dropped the blouse to her side with a heavy sigh. "Batton Deats is just about the worst person to have ever lived in Sugar Cove."

"According to…?"

"Me."

"He can't be that bad."

"He is."

"Why's that?" When Shelby didn't answer, Reece folded her arms. "I'm not letting this go until you tell me everything."

"All right." She turned back to the clothing, but her anger had cooled and she pushed the clothes aside, but this time slower, taking a moment to actually glance at each blouse before moving on to the next. "He was my first boyfriend."

Reece's heart nearly skidded to a stop. "We've talked about boyfriends before, and you've never mentioned him."

"For good reason."

"That being?"

She paused, her gaze skimming a cream-colored shirt. "Because he broke my heart, is why. He broke my heart and left this town, leaving me behind."

"I don't understand. Had he asked you to move with him?"

"More than that," Shelby replied, sucking in a breath. "He proposed and then broke off our engagement, abandoning me."

"I'm so sorry."

"It's okay." Anger flashed in her eyes. "But if there's one thing I know, it's this—if I never see Batton Deats again, I'll be the happiest girl alive."

CHAPTER 5

Ginny

The next morning the phone rang bright and early. Ginny grabbed the landline from where it was attached to the wall. "Hello?"

"This is Mrs. Travis. We met yesterday."

"Good morning, Mrs. Travis. What can I do for you at"—her gaze darted to the clock, and she blanched—"at seven o'clock on a Saturday?"

"I was going to have my assistant call you," the old woman spat, "but she had to visit some family, so I'm calling myself. I would like to meet at ten a.m. Monday morning to discuss the details of you catering the Teal Scarf event."

"Our first dining service is at eleven. That's cutting it a bit close for me to return in time to help with lunch."

"Do you want the business or don't you?"

Of course she did. "Can we meet at the café?"

"You will come to where I am staying."

So much for meeting at the lighthouse. "Yes, ma'am. And where is that?"

Mrs. Travis gave her the address and they said goodbye. When Ginny hung up, she wasn't sure if catering for the woman's event would be such a good idea after all.

* * *

Aiden picked her up an hour before sunset in his truck. It wasn't brand-new, which suited him—worn and comfortable but still rugged.

"Where are we going?" she asked shyly as he opened the door for her.

He quirked a brow. "It's a surprise."

She giggled. "A surprise?"

"That's right."

She turned toward him, the backs of her legs bumping into the truck's frame. "Are you going to blindfold me?"

"Do you want me to?"

Her cheeks warmed. "No, but that would make sure I'm never able to retrace my footsteps and find the place again."

He took a step closer. Unsure of what to do with her hands, she gripped the door handle. Aiden took another step and her breath hitched. The air between them filled with tension—the good kind, the kind that occurred right before a kiss.

She licked her lips, and his gaze flickered to her mouth. He dropped his voice. "What if I want you to be able to find where I'm taking you? So that you can return anytime you want?"

"Well...then..." What should she say? Her mind had gone blank. Thoughts weren't coming. All she could think about were his lips and how they would feel against hers, and what his kiss would taste like. "Well, then, I suppose I would like that."

Her response was so terrible that Ginny felt like her brain had betrayed her.

But Aiden didn't seem to notice the lack of witty banter. He only smiled, which was like looking into the sun, blinding and happy. "Let's get going. We don't want to be late."

She slid onto the seat. "For what?"

"The sunset."

* * *

They drove to a marina, where Aiden parked, and from there they got into his boat.

Being nosy, she peeked into the built-in cooler. "You've brought food."

He glanced over his shoulder, chuckling. "I wasn't going to take you to see the most perfect sunset and let you starve."

"You are quite thoughtful."

He laughed harder. "And you are quite funny."

Their gazes locked and tension charged the air again until Ginny, who felt like an electrical bolt was spider-crawling down her spine, cleared her throat and took a seat by Aiden.

"Now will you tell me where we're going?"

"Not until we get there."

"Does your radio work in case you run out of gas?"

He frowned. "You really aren't sure how to have fun, are you?"

She shook her head and leaned back on the white leather seat. "I guess I'm still figuring that out. Being married for a long time, especially to a man as staunch as Jack was, still clings to me. It's hard to let loose."

"I'm sorry."

"It's not your fault."

They were silent while he steered the boat from the marina and into the emerald waters of the Gulf. "For what it's worth, I know what it is to have some of the fun sucked from your life."

"You? The treasure hunter? How is that possible?" she joked.

He only scowled at her playfully. "I was married too, you know. Not that I'm saying marriage can be bad. We were very happy in the beginning."

"I remember that you're divorced," she replied, feeling like a jerk for suggesting he didn't feel as deeply as she did. "I didn't mean to offend you."

"You didn't. Come here and let me show you how to steer."

"Are you serious?"

"Do I look like I'm joking?" He frowned, which made her laugh. "Come."

She reluctantly slid from the seat and made her way over. Aiden released his left hand and stepped away, giving her room to station herself behind the wheel. He kept his right hand where it was until she had taken her spot. Then he released his hand and she placed hers on the warm metal, where his had been.

She expected him to move away, but he didn't. He remained behind her, his mouth beside her ear, his breath tickling the fine hairs around it. If she'd wanted to, Ginny could have leaned back to sink onto his chest.

"Keep your hands steady like that. Good."

His breath in her ear made a tingle shimmy down her spine all the way to her toes. Her heart slammed against her chest, and she knew that her face was a glorious shade of embarrassed crimson.

"Now what do I do?" she asked.

"Just what you are. I'll tell you when to turn."

His right arm reached around her, and his fingers brushed her hand. A bolt of energy sizzled up her arm. "Keep your grip strong. Good."

"I'm so nervous."

"There's no need to be. I've got you."

It felt like he meant more than just steering. He was there to support her if she wanted it. All she had to do was let him in.

"Tell me what happened with your ex-wife. I've told you about Jack, what he did to my family. I'd like to hear about her."

"Well," he started slowly, his breath sending shudders down her spine, "we were young when we married. I'd known her a long time before that, though, so no big deal. But after we'd been married a few years, we discovered that she couldn't have children."

"I'm sorry."

"It's okay. I wanted to adopt, and she didn't, and she was sad for a long time. I helped her through it as much as I could. She went to a therapist, and I thought she was getting better, but that sorrow turned into a spending habit."

That was surprising. "She spent money as grieving."

"Yeah, but it was more than that. It was like she had thrown herself entirely into having a baby, and when she couldn't have one, she had to throw herself into something else—and that was shopping.

Ginny"—the sound of her name on his lips made her heart leap into her throat—"she would spend thousands in a month on decorations for the house, or new clothes for me and for her. As soon as I made the money, she was spending it. So I talked to her about it. We went to counseling together, but I couldn't let her destroy our lives with her habits. We started fighting—a lot, and that fighting led her into the arms of another man."

"Oh, Aiden."

"It's okay. I've dealt with it."

"But still, that's so hard. I can't imagine. Well, I can actually."

He squeezed her left arm. "We've both been hurt by our ex-spouses."

She expected him to pull his hand away, but he didn't. Instead Aiden made small circles with his thumb, warming her exposed flesh. His other hand rested on her right shoulder, and Ginny didn't dare breathe. She hadn't been this close to a man in months, and she hadn't been close like this to anyone expect Jack in over twenty years.

"We're here," he said suddenly, and her heart dropped.

She hadn't known what she expected or wanted from Aiden. His closeness made her squirm, but it also felt right, which surely had to be wrong. She needed time to adjust to the idea of a new man.

He pointed, and before them stretched a long finger of land with a sandy beach. Behind the beach lay a long strip of grassy land. There wasn't a house or a person in sight.

"What is this place?"

"St. Vincent Island," he said, taking a step back.

A breath loosened inside her chest and Ginny exhaled. "I've never heard of it."

"It's an uninhabited island. People can come shelling and for picnics, but not to live."

"No one will be around?"

He moved to where she could see him, and he smiled. "No one."

"You're not going to take advantage of me, are you?"

He barked a laugh. "I could ask you the same thing."

"Don't worry," she replied with a giggle. "You're safe with me."

"As are you with me."

He said it quietly, and their gazes latched onto one another again. That tension loomed and Ginny glanced back down at her hands.

"Are you going to tell me how to park this thing?"

He grinned. "I sure will."

After they had pulled up to a swath of grassy land where they were able to drop anchor, Aiden helped her and a huge wicker basket from the boat.

"What all do you have in that thing?"

"You'll see," he teased. "And no peeking."

She lifted her hands in surrender. "You can count on me. I won't sneak one peek."

They walked down a grassy path until they were on the beach proper. Sand stretched for hundreds of yards to the left, and waves gently lapped at the shore.

Behind them, small grassy dunes jutted up from the earth, and crab holes pockmarked the sand.

"This is beautiful," she told him, sucking in a breath.

"Just wait. It's about to get even more beautiful." The way he looked at her, with his eyes shining, made her think that Aiden wasn't only talking about the beach or the sunset that was to come. "Here. Let me get this blanket out."

"You stuffed a blanket in the basket?"

"Of course. Where else would I put it?"

She laughed as he wrestled out a blanket that had been tightly stuffed into the basket and spread it along the beach.

They sat as the sun dipped into the horizon. The sky became washed in gold, peach and magenta.

Aiden made her a plate of fried chicken, watermelon salad topped with feta cheese, and apple-cider cole slaw.

"That looks yummy. Who's your chef?"

"I'll never tell."

She elbowed him. "Seriously."

He nodded. "Seriously. I never reveal my sources. All you need to know is that you're having dinner with a handsome man on the beach."

She hooted with laughter. "Handsome? You think awfully highly of yourself."

"I am having dinner with a beautiful woman, so that means I also think highly of you."

Her heart jackhammered against her ribs again and Ginny's cheeks flushed. There were no words on her tongue. Not one. So she focused on the food and returned to the story of his ex-wife.

"Your wife...you divorced her after you caught her cheating?"

Aiden's eyes snapped as if he'd been thinking of something completely different. He stretched his legs out in front of him and nodded.

"Yep. She told me that she'd found someone else, so I had the papers drawn up. Since she'd cheated and admitted it, I didn't have to pay alimony, and she took up real estate. She's one of the most successful agents around."

Her jaw dropped. "She still lives here?"

"Sure does. We run into each other from time to time."

"And is she still with that man?"

"They married, then divorced. She's been single ever since, I think."

His shoulders tightened and Ginny frowned. "You're hiding something."

His gaze swiveled from the horizon to meet hers. "What makes you say that?"

"You're tense. There's more to the story. Aiden, if there's one thing I've learned in the past months, it's to trust my instincts."

He studied her a moment and sighed. "Yeah, I see Jennifer every once in a while."

"And..."

"And she keeps trying to get back together, but I'm not interested. There's someone else I'd rather spend my time with."

He looked at her with such intensity then that Ginny felt the world drop away. She was floating, or drowning in emotion, she didn't know which, until something large, brown, furry and buzzing flew directly into her face.

She reared back and screamed. "Ah!"

Aiden jumped up. "What the...? It's a carpenter bee. It won't hurt you. Just sit still and it'll go away."

The gigantic bumblebee thing zoomed around Ginny as if it wanted to eat her. After a moment it flew off, only to be replaced by another, even hairier bee. She yelped again.

That one landed on her shoulder. She froze.

"Don't move," Aiden told her calmly. "It'll go in a minute."

She stayed still as a stick until the bee buzzed off.

After that one zoomed away, three more launched themselves at the couple, hovering and buzzing inches from their faces.

They were so close that Ginny cringed. She moved toward Aiden, burying her face in his shoulder.

"Please tell me when it's gone."

"It's just curious. You look like a flower to it."

"I don't want to look like a flower."

She could hear the smile in his voice when he replied, "You can't help what you are."

What did that mean? But his words weren't what grabbed her attention. What did was his delicious scent. Aiden smelled of the briny ocean mixed with musk. The smell instantly soothed her even if the death knell of a buzzing carpenter bee was blaring in her ears.

"Is it safe?"

He was cupping her head. When had that happened?

"They're gone," he whispered.

She tipped her face back and stared up into his blue eyes flecked with gold, the look in them as tumultuous as the roaring ocean itself.

Her breath caught in the back of her throat. She swallowed a knot and said in a whisper, "Do you think they'll come back?"

"I don't know."

Then he dipped his head and every part of Ginny screamed not to kiss him, that she wasn't ready. But at the same time every other part of her cried out for his lips.

Just as their lips were inches from touching, a big brown bee buzzed between them.

Ginny threw up her arms and screamed. She stumbled back and

Aiden caught her hand, grabbing her before she could fall onto the sand.

The bee flew off and he watched it. When he looked back at her, he said, "Want to go?"

Fear clung to her like yesterday's underwear. "Yes."

He nodded. "Let me just gather everything up."

As they walked back to the boat, Ginny wondered if she'd just blown things with Aiden for good.

CHAPTER 6
Ginny

"And then carpenter bees attacked," she told her daughters and Hudson at brunch the next morning. "They were this big"—she made a wide space between her thumb and forefinger—"and they wanted revenge for what humans have done in the past."

Reece laughed. "They did not want revenge."

Ginny dropped her hand atop the table. "They didn't say as much, but I know the truth."

Chandler tore a hunk of bread from the French baguette they were dipping into seasoned oil. "If they'd wanted that much revenge, they would've followed you home."

"I concur," Hudson said.

She shrugged. "I'm only telling you what I know. But enough about me—how's wedding planning going?"

"Good." Her daughter shrugged. "I'm calling places to find a venue. It depends on their availability as to when the date will actually be."

Ginny glanced out toward the ocean, at the water slapping against the sugary sand "Why don't you have it here?"

Hudson glanced expectantly at Chandler. "I like that idea. What do you think?"

One side of her mouth ticked up. "That's great. Then we can have the wedding whenever we want."

"You can." Ginny rose and crossed to the window. "We can set up chairs just off the deck and the ceremony can take place right on the beach. There's plenty of room, depending on how many people you invite."

"I'd like to keep it small," her daughter admitted.

"My mother may want to make it big, but she'll go along with whatever you say," Hudson told her with a squeeze of her hand before glancing at his watch. "Looks like I've got to head out. I'm meeting with the senior partners of the firm before I start."

"You're leaving so soon," she said.

"I hate to eat and run." He rose and kissed the top of Chandler's head. "But duty calls."

"I understand," Ginny told him.

As soon as Hudson left, Reece pounced. "How does he like it here? Does he hate it? Is it way too laid back for him?"

"Whoa, tiger," her sister joked. "He likes it, but Hudson's used to having the world at his doorstep, so that's been a learning curve. In the past he would eat out every night, but now he's learning to cook."

Reece's eyes widened. "A lawyer learning to cook? What's he made so far, ramen noodles?"

She wadded up her napkin and tossed it at her sister. "Very funny. No. He's grilled hamburgers." The three women exchanged a look before bursting into laughter. "What? Don't hamburgers count as cooking?"

"They do, honey, they do. They count more than you know."

"Yeah, first it's burgers and before you know it, he'll be making his own fancy mayonnaises."

"Stop it, Reece," Chandler scolded, knuckling tears of laughter from her eyes.

"A new life means big changes," Ginny told them. "He loves you very much to have moved here."

"I know." Her voice and her gaze dropped. "He does."

Reece and Ginny exchanged a look. It was her youngest who spoke. "What's wrong? Why the long face?"

"It's nothing."

She wasn't buying it. "It's definitely not nothing. What's going on, honey? You can tell us."

Chandler raked her fingers through her hair and exhaled a loud sigh, slumping down onto her chair. "Everything was good until... until I started to think about Daddy and what he did to you."

"Okay...what does that have to do with anything?"

"You don't think...it's just that...how do I make sure that doesn't happen to me?"

Her words were a sucker punch to the throat. "Oh. Well. I guess that I don't know. Wait. Hudson loves you. Why are you thinking these things?"

"I shouldn't be."

"No, you shouldn't," Reece agreed in a flinty voice. "What Daddy did happened to Mama, not you."

"I know. It's true." She slowly lifted her gaze to meet Ginny's, and pain filled her eyes. "It's just that I can't help wondering if that's in my future, too."

She yearned to tell her daughter that of course history wouldn't repeat itself, that what had happened to her would never happen to Chandler. But how could she make a promise that wasn't hers to keep? Yet the pain and worry in her daughter's eyes were real, and both needed to be tended. If they weren't, the worry would only fester and become worse.

"No one knows what the future holds," she said slowly, trying to quickly pluck the best word choice from her brain. "But what I can tell you is that your father and Hudson are very different men. Jack was always selfish, even from the beginning. He was someone caught up in society and making sure his image was perfect. Hudson, though I don't know him as well as you, doesn't seem to be that way. He seems like a kind, thoughtful man who's putting your needs ahead of his own. Would Jack have ever moved to the beach for me before we were married? I doubt it. He would've released me rather than track me down. Put all those fears aside. They won't do anything except rot the great relationship you've got."

A wobbly smile alighted on Chandler's face. The worry still

flashed in her eyes, but Ginny could tell that she had listened, and that the seed of her words could begin to sprout and hopefully strangle the other weeds of thought that were trying to take root.

"Mama's right," Reece said. "Hudson isn't Daddy, so don't make him be like that."

"I know he's not, but I said yes to marrying him, and now all this doubt is creeping into my mind. I don't want to be this way. I don't want to think this, but how can I not? Not after what just happened to you, Mama. It's not like any of us ever expected that Daddy would have a second family and he'd take the house from you, but he did. And now I'm about to start my life with Hudson, and Daddy's shadow is hanging over that."

Ginny's heart ached for her daughter. "Have you talked to Hudson about this?"

"No."

"You should. You need to tell him your worries and your doubts. If you don't, they'll become a wedge between you. He won't know what's wrong, and you'll be afraid to tell him. If Jack had come to me years earlier and asked for a divorce, it would've been hard, but I would have managed it. Actually I would have preferred that to learning about his secret life when the will was read."

Reece threw up her arms. "But then you wouldn't have bought the lighthouse."

She tossed her head back and laughed. "No, I wouldn't have, and I wouldn't have started my own business—with the help of my two wonderful daughters." Her gaze nestled onto Chandler, who still looked lost. Ginny wished for the time when her daughter was still young, when she would hold her close, run her fingers through her hair and whisper in her ear that everything would be okay. But those days were long gone, and deep rips had torn her heart since then. "Talk to him. Talk to Hudson and let him know your worries. I guarantee that he'll understand, and he'll be thankful you told him."

She inhaled deeply. "You're right. I'll tell him."

"Good."

"Great." Reece slapped her hands together. "If we're done, I need to get prepping for tomorrow's lunch. We're having fried chicken, potato salad and creamy cole slaw."

Ginny rose. "Oh, that reminds me—I'm meeting with Mrs. Travis in the morning."

"Mrs. Who?"

"Travis. She's an older woman who wants us to cater a luncheon for her. I may be a bit late getting back."

"That's okay." Her youngest loaded plates onto her hand. "Chandler will be here to help."

"Actually I might not be," she said with a grimace. "I promised Vicki that I'd help move some things around at the studio. But I can ask her to reschedule."

"No, that's okay. I can handle lunch by myself for a few minutes. No big deal."

Ginny frowned. "You sure?"

"Yeah."

Reece flashed her a wide smile full of straight, white teeth. She was so pretty. Her beauty wasn't like Chandler's, who had been gifted with a long, lithe body, hair the color of a wheat field, and bright eyes. No, Reece was more of the girl-next-door type with her brown hair and round cheeks. She was approachable, sweet, whereas Chandler was untouchable. Reece never appreciated her own looks, though, but Ginny did.

"I got this," her youngest insisted. "But only if you promise to read that diary and tell us what it says."

She sighed. "Fine. I'll start it tonight, and I'll let you know everything that's in it."

"Thank you."

As she helped her daughters clear the table, her phone buzzed. A wistful smile played on her face. It was probably Aiden calling to see if she'd recovered from the bees. But when she glanced at the name on the screen, her heart dropped.

She recognized the number immediately because it had been the landline in her old home, the fabulous house in Buckhead, the home of her dreams—or nightmares, now.

Only one person could have been calling her from that number—Savannah, Jack's mistress, and the woman who now lived her old life.

"Who is it, Mama?" Chandler asked. "You're staring at that phone as if it's a ghost."

Ginny bristled. She dropped the phone into her pocket as if it were a hot potato. "It's no one. Just a spam call."

It was no one, indeed.

CHAPTER 7
Emma Grace

I am in love. It sounds so silly to say, so childish, but it's true. Diary, I met him today, the man I will marry. Only he isn't a man yet. But he will soon be.

Papa has secured the job at the new lighthouse. It's a fine place with bigger rooms than the last one. Now I have a bedroom all to myself.

We had only just settled in when Papa sent me to get flour and coffee from the store.

There aren't many shops here. It's mostly small houses along the sandy road. The town is small but growing. I found the general store easily enough and purchased what Papa had asked for. I'd only just paid and was leaving, walking out the door, when I dropped my wallet. Before I could grab it, a strong hand with thick muscles took it first.

I looked up into the brightest eyes I've ever seen. They were flecked with brown and so warm. There stood a young man who was taller than me, with strong shoulders and dark brown hair. He smiled and handed me the wallet.

"You dropped this."

"Thank you." I couldn't even look at him he was so beautiful.

"I haven't seen you before. Are you new?"

I told him my name and we'd just moved here, but that Papa had lived in the area before.

"I'm James but everybody calls me Jim. Maybe I'll see you again, then," he said before going into the store.

Diary, I couldn't breathe when I walked away. I just hope that I'll see him again. I can't imagine not ever looking at that face once more.

* * *

Diary, I have seen him. I was coming home from school (I have one year left), when I saw Jim walking down the road. He spotted me and he smiled. Diary, he smiled and said, "Well, if it isn't Emma Grace, the lighthouse keeper's daughter."

My cheeks burned so hot when he said that, and I became so nervous that I was sure I wouldn't be able to say anything, but somehow I managed to reply, "It's not fair that you know who I am, and I don't know about your father."

"Oh, my father?" He stared down at me with eyes that made me stop breathing. Then he rubbed the back of his neck shyly. "My father's a fisherman. He catches the biggest red snapper you've ever seen. Caught one as big as a whale once, but the fish sweet-talked him into being thrown back in."

I laughed and Jim asked if he could escort me somewhere. I told him that I was going home, and he asked to walk me there.

"You're not even going that way," I told him.

"What if I am now?"

"If you're sure, then you may walk me."

"Such nice manners. I'm not sure that I'm fit company to be in the presence of a fine lady."

"Then perhaps you should keep walking," I joked, and he laughed.

Oh, Diary! I can't tell you all that we talked about because my mind is still spinning from it. But I found out that his name is James (I already knew that, of course. See? I still can't think straight), he's from here, and in a year he hopes to have saved enough money to leave. His father desperately wants him to be a fisherman, but Jim doesn't want to do that. He wants to move to a big city and start a business. He doesn't know what kind, but something that doesn't involve fish. He told me so much that I asked him why he was sharing all of it.

He shrugged. "I don't know. There's something kind in you, Emma Grace, and my heart says it's okay to tell you about me."

By then I was home, and so he left. But he asked if it would be okay to take me to the movies, and of course I told him that I had to ask my father. Then I came straight here to write everything down. Now all I have to do is tell Papa.

* * *

Terrible news, Diary. I told Papa about Jim, and he said the worst thing that I could ever hear.

"You stay away from that boy and his family."

"But I don't understand. Why?"

"Just do as I say," he yelled, really *yelled. "Do it and don't question me."*

Then he opened the whiskey bottle and took a long drink like he does when he's worried, and at that point I knew the conversation was over. There would be no talking to him about Jim because his mind was made up. But why? Why was he acting like that? He doesn't even know Jim, so what could he have ever done against Papa?

* * *

Diary, I've tried to put him out of my head, I really have. I've tried and tried. I've studied more, I've even met a few girls who are nice, but try as I may, Jim is still in my thoughts.

And I've been seeing him in secret.

It's terrible, a horrible thing to do behind Papa's back. I planned on obeying him, I swear. But then I saw Jim.

He showed up outside the school on Monday. I'd told him that if I could meet him on Saturday for a movie, that I would see him at the theater. But since that day had come and gone, I figured he'd think that I wasn't interested in him. Even thinking that makes my heart ache, Diary. It's like I've known him all my life, and I don't want to hurt him.

But he was standing outside the school with a lopsided grin on his face. "You missed a great movie. Shane *will go down in the history books.*"

He said it in a teasing way, and I couldn't help but to laugh. "Do you like Westerns?"

"As much as you do."

I cocked my head. "How do you know I like Westerns? I could prefer space alien movies."

He laughed. "A lighthouse girl dreaming of space aliens? I don't think so. You'd rather be living an adventure in the Old West, donning a cowgirl hat and riding a bucking bronco."

It was my turn to laugh, which broke the tension between us. "I'm sorry about Saturday."

"Me too. Why didn't you come?"

How could I tell him what Papa had said? "I, um, had to do some things for my father. The lighthouse is a mess and needs a lot of cleaning."

He looked at me then, and Diary, I swear it felt like he was looking straight into my soul. "You don't have to lie. If you didn't want to go, just tell me."

My heart nearly stopped beating then. He was looking at me with such intention that my gaze fell to the ground. "I...I do want to see you, but my father won't allow it."

"Ah, I understand. The fisherman's son isn't good enough for the lighthouse keeper's daughter."

He started to walk away, and panic spread through my body. I grabbed his sleeve. "It's not like that." He halted and turned around, his shoulder slumping in defeat. "I don't know why he doesn't want me to see you. He won't say."

"Maybe I should meet him."

"No!" Then quieter I said, "I don't think that would help."

Jim tipped his head and studied me. It felt like I was an onion and every part of me was made up of layers. His eyes seemed to peel back those layers, one at a time, exposing me in a way that frightened and excited me.

"What do you want to do?" he asked.

I bit my bottom lip and thought about it. "I don't want to go against my father."

"You're sixteen, practically a woman."

"I know." *I kicked a pebble out of my path.* "But he's still my father."

"I understand." *He took a step back and started to turn again.*

"But I want to see you," *I added.*

He stopped and pivoted back to face me. "Are you sure?"

And then Diary, I said the boldest thing that I've ever said in my life, because it goes against what I'm supposed to do.

I remember lifting my head, feeling every ounce of defiance vibrating in my bones when I answered, "Yes, I'm sure that I want to see you."

And so now I have a secret boyfriend. I pray that Papa never finds out.

CHAPTER 8
Ginny

The home where Mrs. Travis was staying was a two-story white home just off the ocean in Port St. Joe. It sat on a square patch of grass that seemed almost out of place so close to the beach.

The home had black shutters and a cupola at the top, giving it a regal look. Ginny glanced down at her flowing dress and sandals and wondered if she should have dressed nicer for the meeting.

Well, it was too late to change her clothes now, so what she wore would have to do.

The door opened as soon as she knocked, and the driver from the other day opened it. "Mrs. Travis is expecting you," he said politely.

Ginny followed him into the home, which was lavishly decorated with expensive rugs on the floors and custom paintings in gilded frames hanging on the walls.

The home was reminiscent of her old house in Buckhead, the one she'd had to abandon. Her stomach twinged in anger, and she exhaled slowly to release the hurt that still sliced sharply through her whenever she thought too much about it.

To distract herself, she focused on the decor. Large potted palms were tucked into the corners, and the crimson rugs were accented with golden drapes and cloths that graced the accent tables sprinkled about the foyer and beyond.

They walked through an open set of glass-lined French doors out into a sunroom. Sunlight splashed onto the white marble tile with ebony veins racing through it. More palms hugged the corners of the room, and a white wrought-iron table was placed in the center of the space, flanked by two matching chairs.

Mrs. Travis sat in one eating what looked like her breakfast. She turned slowly and greeted Ginny with a nod.

"Good to see you again. Can Sam bring you anything?"

"Tea would be appreciated." She had learned a long time ago that when someone offered you a refreshment, it was best to take it. "Unsweetened is fine."

"Very well." Mrs. Travis flicked her hand and he left. "Sam'll be back in a moment."

Mrs. Travis was dressed in a sea-green suit dress with a white silk blouse peeking out underneath it. She pinned her stony gaze on Ginny, which caused a flush to work up her neck. It had been a long time since she'd been in the presence of a woman like this—powerful, able to twirl her finger and have anything and everything done, but Ginny wouldn't cower, even if the woman's eyes looked like they were seeing straight through her.

"Thank you for coming."

"You're very welcome. We're excited for the opportunity to host the Teal Scarf Ladies."

"We do a lot of charity work, you know," Mrs. Travis explained. "We help women and children in the community. Well, most of them do. I only oversee. I don't live here full-time. Much of my time is spent in Atlanta."

"You don't say. That's where I moved from."

"What area?"

"Buckhead." Mrs. Travis's eyebrows lifted. "It's a long story," she told her with a wave of her hand. "I'm happy here."

"I haven't been to Sugar Cove in…a long time. But when the president of the Teal Scarves suggested that we have the annual meeting here, I couldn't say no. Though I wanted to."

Her brows rose. Ginny fought the urge to ask such a personal question as to why Mrs. Travis wanted to say no, but she kept her mouth shut.

"I lived here, but that was way back before you were ever born. The rest of my life has been spent in the city, and my husband was a very successful businessman. He owned one of the local television stations for years until he sold it."

That explained the wealth. "My late husband was also very successful."

"I assumed so," Mrs. Travis snipped. "You don't look like you've worked in a kitchen all your life."

"What do you mean?"

Her gaze flicked to Ginny's hands. "Your fingers aren't cracked and flat from pounding or cutting. Your face looks too well pampered. Tell me—do you miss your monthly facials?"

Ginny nearly choked on the sip of tea that Sam had dropped off a few seconds before. She cleared her throat. "I've found that life here is much simpler than it was back in Atlanta. I prefer it."

The older woman nodded as if that was answer enough, while Ginny started to wonder if she'd bitten off more than she could chew working with this woman.

"Tell me, what ideas do you have for the luncheon?" Mrs. Travis asked.

She didn't have any, expecting that the older woman would know what menu she wanted, which meant that she needed to come up with something quick. "We could do a choice of seafood and chicken, since some people have allergies to shellfish. Perhaps a chicken in wine sauce and maybe either shrimp and grits or perhaps West Indies Crab salad? Or a crab pie?"

"I prefer West Indies, don't you? Such a delightful and delicate dish, very apropos for the region. And if you're going that route, perhaps you could make Lane Cake for dessert."

Ginny nearly blanched. She'd never made Lane Cake. It was a three-tiered white cake with vanilla frosting. That was the simple part. Between the layers were raisins, coconut, and the cake was brushed with bourbon. Reece would love making it, she was sure. But it was so complicated that they would need a practice run.

"Lane Cake? That's quite—"

"Southern," Mrs. Travis finished with a wide smile and glittering eyes. She stabbed into a sausage link and took a delicate bite, chewing before adding, "It would definitely fit with the theme for this year. I expect that the rest of the menu you can fill out yourself. With one cold dish and one hot dish, the sides should be easy—green beans, perhaps a carrot salad, maybe frozen cranberry salad, simple things that are easy for you to put together."

"Certainly," Ginny said. A long stretch of silence ignited between them, which she took as her hint to leave. "I'll just put together a menu and send it over."

"Fine. Then we'll do a tasting beforehand."

"Of course. Will you want to do that her—"

"Do you like living in the lighthouse?"

The question took her off guard. Her eyes flared and then narrowed. "Yes, I do. I live there with my daughters."

"The two young women who I saw at the café?"

"Yes. My youngest bakes, and my oldest is a jewelry designer. She moved down from New York."

"Sugar Cove certainly is a magical place." Her eyes shimmered with memories. "It holds special meaning for many people."

"Do you...do you have fond memories of the lighthouse?"

"What?" she blinked. "Oh yes. It's quite the spectacle, don't you think? We'd race along the beach and see the lighthouse towering over the sand. And when that light would shine at night, oh that was a sight."

"Who was the keeper when you were young?" Perhaps this woman had known Emma Grace. Maybe she could shed some light as to what had happened to her.

"I don't recall his name."

"Was there an Emma Grace here?"

Mrs. Travis's jaw slackened. "Why yes, there was."

"There's a story that she disappeared."

Sadness filled the old woman's eyes. "It's tragic, what happened."

Ginny's fingers curled and uncurled anxiously. "What did happen?"

"If I recall, there was a storm. Emma Grace raced out into it, and it's believed she drowned."

Her heart sank. "Oh, I see."

"Why do you ask?"

For some reason she couldn't bring herself to reveal anything about the diary. Doing so felt like a betrayal to Emma Grace, even though she was long dead. "I was just curious. We've heard stories, is all, and I had hoped that perhaps she had lived."

"No, no. No body was ever discovered. She wasn't found."

Her heart grew heavy hearing that. "I see."

"Is there anything else that I can tell you about Sugar Cove? Any of its history that you'd like to know more about?"

"No, I think that's it." She glanced down at her watch and saw that it was already well past ten, going on eleven. Her heart fluttered. She needed to get back to the café. Reece was probably having a heck of a time with the lunch rush. "Thank you for the tea. I need to be heading back."

Mrs. Travis flicked her finger, and the driver appeared at her side. How did she do that? "Sam will show you out."

Ginny nearly ran to the front door. All she could think about as she slid into the front seat of her car was that Reece was probably going to kill her for being so late.

CHAPTER 9
Reece

Monday morning dawned and the sun remained hidden behind a bank of clouds. It wouldn't rain, the forecast had promised, but the sun wouldn't show itself until later in the morning.

That didn't matter to Reece, who was busy making the last preparations before the lunch service began. Mondays were generally busy. It seemed that all of Sugar Cove (and the next towns over) spent their weekends depressed that the café was closed for two days. To make up for it, they stormed the doors as soon as it opened.

The day's menu was an easy one—chicken and dumplings with green beans and a salad, along with banana pudding for dessert. The salads were made, and all Reece had to do was scoop out the main dishes and place them on plates, as well as grab drinks for the guests.

When she opened the doors at eleven, there was a line of people longer than Reece expected. She blanched but managed to swallow down the panic scrambling up her throat and started seating guests.

But folks were pouring into the café faster than Reece could keep up. She usually plated food while her mother grabbed drinks. Chandler moved back and forth between the kitchen and dining room, helping out wherever she was needed.

But with twenty drink orders, food to plate, and another ten folks just walking in the door, Reece's face was on fire with anxiety.

She couldn't keep up. She couldn't deliver drinks, plate the food, welcome people and get everything done in a jiffy.

She'd just sat the last table and was preparing to head into the kitchen to somehow make thirty drinks and prepare food when a deep Southern drawl said from behind her, "You look like you could use some help."

She turned and there stood Ted, all broad shoulders, sparkling eyes and sandy hair. His brow was wrinkled in concern, which Reece found adorable even though she should've been freaking out about being overwhelmed at the café.

"Where's your help?" he asked.

Reece blinked. Oh, that's right. She was supposed to talk to him, to respond. "They, uh, had stuff." They had *stuff*? Wow. She was never going to win conversationalist of the year with replies like that.

He rolled up his sleeves, revealing droolworthy muscled forearms. "Let me help."

She wanted to laugh. It was the most absurd request ever—Ted helping her through the first lunch service. But as Reece glanced around and spotted folks drumming their fingers impatiently, she realized his offer was a blessing.

"Okay, come and help. Be sure to wash your hands first."

"I've been in a kitchen or two," he said, not unkindly.

After Ted washed his hands, she steered him to the food warmers. "Every person gets a plate that has one scoop of chicken and dumplings and one scoop of green beans. Then you also give them a salad, they're here"—she pointed to the refrigerator—"there are thirty folks out there. I'll get the drinks while you plate the food."

"Got it," he said with a smile. "Should I put on a hair net?"

Even though he was serious, she couldn't help but smile. "I think your hair is short enough that you don't need one."

He clapped his hands. "Let's get to it."

As Reece poured sweet teas, Ted diligently did as she'd told him, making plate after plate of food. When there wasn't any more room on the counter for plates of chicken and dumplings, he said, "Let me take these out. Who do they go to?"

"Everyone."

As he picked up plates and moved past her, she continued pouring drinks until the guests were served. Then she delivered plates that Ted was making.

She'd pick them up and return, saying, "We need ten more," then that become, "six more," and finally, "two more and it's time to move to dessert."

His brows rose. "Dessert?"

She laughed. "You've eaten here before; you know how it goes. Everyone gets dessert."

"You got it, boss."

Once all the main courses were out, Reece opened the big refrigerator door. "Here's dessert, already dished up."

The banana puddings were dropped into small glass dessert bowls with slender stems and were each topped with fresh whipped cream.

"My stomach's rumbling just looking at these," he told her with a wink.

Her own stomach flip-flopped. "No time to eat yet, mister. We've got customers."

"Yes, ma'am," he joked, but Reece couldn't tamp down her wide grin.

What was she doing? Ted was off-limits. But right now he was saving her from a disastrous lunch service, so she was thankful.

When all the banana puddings were delivered, she sat on a stool in the kitchen with a heavy sigh. Ted joined her and crossed his arms.

"It's been a long time since I've worked that hard in a kitchen," he confessed.

She quirked a brow. "You've worked in a kitchen?"

"Oh yeah. I worked in the bar's kitchen, saved my money and was friends with the owner." He glanced away, giving Reece an excellent view of his profile. It was impossible *not* to admire it. "The owner never had a son, and so he took me under his wing, and when he was ready to sell the place, he gave it to me for a steal."

"I didn't know that."

He nodded. "Well, we never went out on that date we were supposed to, so how could you?"

His voice teased, but his eyes were serious. Heat creeped up her cheeks, and shame burned in her gut. "Right. Well, my loss, right?"

Before he could answer, she jumped up, "I bet folks are ready to check out."

He rose as well. "What do you need me to do?"

"Clear plates?" she asked bashfully, hating to put him to even more work when he'd done so much already. "I'll ring people up."

"It would be my pleasure," he practically purred, which made a shiver rock down her spine. It was wrong how her body reacted to this guy. Just wrong.

She swallowed in a poor attempt to put moisture back in her dry mouth and headed out to take payment from customers.

While she did so, every few moments her gaze would land on Ted, who was bussing tables like a pro. Where had he found the rag to wipe them down?

He looked up from where he hovered over a table, and his gaze locked on hers. Though her first instinct was to look away, instead Reece smiled.

And Ted smiled back.

Her heart stuttered and she only ripped her gaze away when the next person in line stepped up to pay their bill.

When it was all said and done and the last person was gone, she slumped onto a cane-backed chair with a loud sigh.

Ted sat across from her, but he didn't slump, nor did he sigh.

She looked at him, really looked at him without fear and trepidation in her heart. "I owe you one."

"You don't owe me anything. It was fun."

A grin spread across her face. "It *was* fun, wasn't it?"

"That's what you live for in this business, the rush. It's fun moving that fast, getting all the food out."

"But it's also good when it's over."

"That is true." He studied her for a moment. "There are a lot of things that I could've been in life. My dad wanted me to be a lawyer like him, but I never wanted that. I wanted to do something else. I suppose it's good he didn't push me too hard into law."

"Your dad, too?"

His brows lifted. "Let me guess—yours had your life all planned out for you, too?"

"I was supposed to be a doctor."

He released a low whistle. "A doctor? You must be smart."

"Hardly." He shot her a skeptical look. "Okay, so I was smart enough to get into med school, but I hated it. Left a few months ago."

"And how'd your father take it?"

She gulped down a knot that had lodged in her throat. "He didn't. He passed away."

"I'm sorry."

She waved him away. "It's okay. Well, it's not, but we're managing." Reece had no intention of going into her father's history with Ted. She hardly knew the man. "If he'd lived, I'm sure he never would've allowed me to quit. Jack Rigby would've marched me back to Tulane, pushed me through the door and locked it behind me."

"Where you would have pined for another life."

A laugh bubbled from her throat. "Exactly."

Their gazes locked and Reece felt something click inside her. It was a feeling that she desperately wished to ignore.

He studied her closely, and it felt like Ted was memorizing her face, noting every freckle that dotted her nose, how one of her earlobes dipped slightly lower than the other. Reece felt completely exposed to his glance, but she didn't care because she was doing the same thing to him, learning the lines that etched his forehead and how the tops of his cheeks were slightly flushed.

"I'd still like to take—"

"I'm back," her mama called as she entered the café.

Reece jumped up from her seat as Ted slowly rose. He clearly didn't feel like they'd just been caught doing something they shouldn't have. Which was how she felt, even though they hadn't done anything inappropriate.

Ginny's gaze darted from her to Ted. "Sorry that I'm late. Did everything go okay?"

"Thanks to Ted." She gestured toward him. "Mama, this is Ted."

"Ted Talmadge, Mrs. Rigby," he said, taking her mother's hand with the backside facing the ceiling and giving it a slight squeeze. "Nice to meet you. I just happened to be in the neighborhood and saw that your daughter could use a hand."

"Is that so?" she replied, widening her eyes at Reece in a look that basically asked if this was the guy she had mentioned before.

"He was a huge help," she confessed. "If Ted hadn't shown up, I would've been underwater."

"It was my pleasure," he told her, a slight smile lifting one corner of his mouth and his eyes holding a warmth that sent a sizzle all the way to her toes. "You're welcome to put me on payroll."

Both women laughed and Ted started to walk out the door. "Wait," Reece said. "You didn't eat lunch."

He winked. "That's okay. I got what I came for."

With that, he said goodbye and slipped out of the café. Her mother frowned. "If he didn't eat, what did he come here to do?"

"I don't know," she replied, even though Reece had the distinct feeling that his visit had very little to do with food and everything to do with her.

CHAPTER 10
Shelby

Ever since she'd bumped into Batton Deats, Shelby had been unable to get that man out of her head. He'd looked exactly the same as he had in high school—ebony hair, sea-blue eyes, strongly defined muscles. Why couldn't he have been balding and out of shape, cursed with a dad body?

Wait. She didn't know if he was a dad or not. He hadn't been wearing a wedding ring, but that didn't mean he wasn't married, actually *wedded* to a woman he'd proposed to.

She huffed and raked her fingers through her hair.

"Everything okay?" her grandmother asked from behind the hot bar.

"It's fine."

"You don't look fine."

The last thing she wanted was for her grandmother to be knotted up with worry. Age was already getting to Vera—she was slowing at a surprising pace. Oh, she was good at hiding it by getting up earlier to cook the breakfast that the gas station served. Shelby was certain her grandmother thought she hadn't noticed, but she had.

She'd been with her grandmother for years, after all. Her parents had died from a car accident when she was eleven, leaving a good-sized life insurance policy that was used to buy the beach house that was under Shelby's name. The home was hers, and the gas station was her grandmother's. But her grandmother wouldn't be able to work it forever, and if she was being honest with herself, Shelby didn't want to work it if her grandmother wasn't there.

"You look like you could use a break, Shel."

"I could."

Vera slowly shuffled over. Her face sagged with fatigue, and her gray hair peeked out from under the white baseball cap she wore every day. "Why don't you go ahead and get out of here?"

"But my relief isn't here yet."

"He should be here any minute now." Sure enough, a black two-door sports car slid into an empty parking spot. "Speak of the devil. Go on, Shelby. Knock off. I'll see you at home."

"You want a ride?"

She waved her hand in annoyance. "It's right across the street."

"Okay then." She slid off the seat behind the counter and stretched her arms over her head. "But if you change your mind, call me. I won't be far away."

"Just go. Get out of here." The words came out gruffly, but a smile lit her eyes. Her grandmother was a big softy on the inside. "See you at supper."

"See you then."

She grabbed her purse and slipped out the door just as her relief, a college student named Ashton, walked in. She nodded to him before hightailing it to her car and driving away.

* * *

She reached Port St. Joe a few minutes later. Shopping downtown always lifted her spirits, and she expected today to be no exception.

Her first stop was a small antique store that featured plenty of furniture, but Shelby wasn't in the mood for furniture.

Her next stop was Vicki Orr Designs. Reece had told her that Chandler was now selling jewelry there. She scanned the window displays, thinking that all the necklaces and rings were wonderful, but they weren't what she was in the mood for either.

And then she reached the hobby store. This was the place she had wanted to go. In the window sat an old race car track from the seventies. Two cars were side by side, a red one and blue one. They weren't moving, but that was only because no one was pumping the gun that would make them whirl along the track.

She pushed open the door and stepped inside. The place smelled like a secondhand store—full of earth and cardboard. There *were* used things here, like the track, but there were also plenty of new delectables.

An electric train chugged along a platform suspended from the ceiling, winding its way through a tunnel to appear on the other side, moving past a line of fake evergreens.

The track hugged the walls and made a loop around the entire store. Just seeing that fire-red engine chugging along its track made Shelby smile.

As much as she loved clothes shopping—and she did—this place held her heart. She hadn't been here in ages, but very little had changed about it.

New buildable models of ships and the latest military aircraft sat on shelves that greeted her. Just past them would be the paint section, and even farther back would be the trains and car tracks, the kind that were hard to find.

"Let me know if I can help you," said a familiar voice from the back.

A bolt of lightning hissed down her spine. No, it couldn't be. She peered around the end of the aisle and spotted Batton sitting behind the counter. His gaze flicked up, and their jaws dropped at the same.

"What are you—" they both said.

Her hands curled into tight fists. "What are you doing here?"

"I work here," he said in an icy voice.

If anyone had reason to have ice in their heart, it was her, not him. "What do you mean, you work here? This isn't your job. You're—"

"An architect."

Her heart squeezed with an ache she hadn't known in years, or at least since the last time Ted had looked at her with eyes of friendship and not the desire she had hoped he'd have for her.

"You became one?" she whispered.

"Told you I would." He drummed his fingers on the counter impatiently. "Is there anything that I can help you find?"

She could not wrap her head around him being here—in *her* store. Well, technically it was *their* store, as this was where they had spent countless afternoons in high school, nerding out over all the hobby stuff.

Her fingers scraped over an electric car box—*Back to the Future* versus *Knight Rider*. She had a feeling that *Back to the Future* would win, even though it would be a very close call.

"I'm browsing," she replied to his earlier question.

His brow rose skeptically. "Just browsing?"

His suggestion burned angrily in her gut. "Yes, I'm just browsing. I can shop here, you know."

"Of course. It's a free country."

"So they tell me."

She moved to the painting aisle, where Batton couldn't see her. Not where she wanted to be. She wanted to be looking at the racetracks—not that she would buy one. But he could see her from there. Even now she felt his laser-beam gaze penetrating the stacks of brushes and canvases to sear into the back of her head.

"How's your grandmother?"

"Good," she replied curtly.

Silence fell on them—the tense, uncomfortable kind. But Shelby wasn't going to let his presence push her out of *her* store.

"How're your parents?" she asked, only to be polite, not because she actually wanted to know.

"Okay."

Her brow curled. "Just okay?"

He sighed heavily, and her heart almost cracked in two. "They're just okay."

"Is that the reason why you're home?"

It sounded like he was flipping madly through a magazine, the pages turning with a fever that meant he couldn't actually be reading what was on those pages. "Do you care?"

His words stabbed her heart. She could say no, that she didn't care, but of course she did. Not that she wanted to admit it. "I asked, didn't I?"

The page turning stopped suddenly. "I'm home because Dad had a heart attack."

Her stomach dropped. Very slowly she creeped down the aisle and peered over the lip, getting a good look at Batton, who already had his gaze trained on her.

Mr. Deats was a kind man, unlike his son. He'd always been nice, welcoming her to their home. A lump knotted up her throat. "Is he...is he okay?"

"He's weak, so I came home to help."

"But you're here."

"Mr. Landon asked me to work for him today. He had some things to do, and Mom told me to get out of the house because I'm driving her crazy."

One side of his mouth quirked up into a smile, and Shelby's traitorous mouth mimicked the move. She quickly turned her lips into a frown.

"I'm sorry about your father. He was always so kind."

"He adored you."

And the knife in her heart twisted a little more. "Tell him I hope he recovers quickly."

"Thank you."

They stared at each other for so long that it started to become uncomfortable, so Shelby turned back into the aisle.

"Why are you in painting?" he asked.

"Because...I've taken it up."

"You always were a terrible liar."

"I'm not lying." She was *so* lying.

He chuckled, which made the tips of her ears burn. She heard the seat scoot back, and before she could flee, Batton was leaning against the aisle, arms and ankles crossed as if it was the most natural thing in the world to lean against a toy hobby aisle.

"I bet you want that *Knight Rider* versus *Back to the Future* car set."

"Do not."

He smirked. "And if I happened to tell you that there was one already open in the back, just dying to be played with, what would you say?"

Desire to get her hands on that gun controller, to squeeze and release it to make her car move, rushed through her. This was her thing now. It wasn't *their* thing anymore.

"I would say," she replied, dancing her fingers over a palette of paints, "that as tempting as it sounds, that's a hard *no*."

He tipped his head, his gaze pinning her in place. It was as if no time had passed between them, how one look from him could make her bones shatter.

"And why would that be a hard pass, when I'm giving you the opportunity to beat me?"

Her mouth had become a desert. "You know why."

"No, I don't."

Her eyes widened. Was he joking? How could he be so callous? Shelby's body stiffened, and her fingers stopped tracking over the various paint sets. "Batton, don't pretend that what happened between us, didn't."

He shrugged. "I'm not pretending anything; I'm just asking you to play a game."

"And in the process, ignoring what happened."

"What *did* happen?"

Icy fury froze her veins. "You know what happened. You were there."

"All I know is that one day you walked out."

Her mouth fell. The nerve of him. "Because of what you did, I walked out."

Confusion filled his eyes. "What I did? What did I do?"

Was he joking? He had very clearly told her that the engagement was off, that they weren't going to be together.

She stepped forward and pressed the tip of her finger into his chest, which was, to her dismay, as hard as marble. "You know what you did, and if you have a memory problem, I suggest you dig deep to figure it out. Play the game by yourself."

Without another word, she turned on her heel and marched out of her favorite shop in all the world, the one place where she had never expected, nor wanted to think about Batton Deats. Not only was he back in town, but he'd stolen her peace of mind.

It was just another thing to never forgive him for.

CHAPTER 11
Chandler

"I think I burned it," Hudson said, cringing.

He stood over the stove staring down at the skillet. Chandler sniffed the air. She'd just walked into his home using the key he'd given her.

Crossing over to him, she peeked around his arm and took a good long look at the two chicken breasts in the skillet. One side was charred black.

Perhaps this was still salvageable. "What do they look like on the other side?" Hudson flipped one over and she grimaced. "Black as well. Maybe we can scrape it off."

He cocked his chin. "These are inedible. I'm not going to ask you to eat something that I wouldn't. No. Maybe we'll order pizza?"

He was trying so hard to cook that it warmed her heart. She took the pan and walked over to the trash, pressed the foot pedal and dumped the chicken into the container.

"Let me show you how to do it."

He slumped against the counter. "I need all the help I can get."

She gazed at him from the corner of her eye. "You've eaten out for years, so you're out of practice."

He lifted an open bottle of beer from the counter and took a sip. "I don't think that I was ever *in* practice."

"Nonsense."

She smiled at him over her shoulder, and he gave her a warm grin in return. "Teach me. I'm yours to command."

A giggle leaped from her throat. "First, you want a medium heat. You don't want the heat on high or else you'll wind up with what you just had."

He put the sweating beer down and moved behind her, placing his hands on her arms. Her entire body stiffened under his touch. She didn't use to be like that, and she didn't know if he noticed.

The chicken sizzled and he murmured in her ear. "I see. That's how you do it, huh?"

She bashfully wiggled out from his grasp. "I can't concentrate if you're whispering sweet nothings in my ear."

He lifted his hands in surrender. "Duly noted. I'll just be over here."

He relaxed his hip against the counter and sipped his beer while she explained how to cook the chicken.

Before it was done a burning smell, a new one, permeated the kitchen.

She sniffed. "Do you smell burning?"

His eyes flared wide in surprise. "The vegetables! They're in the oven. Stand back."

She took a step back while he grabbed an oven mitt and pulled open the door. A thick cloud of smoke rolled out from the mouth of the oven and swallowed his face.

When he reappeared, Hudson shut the oven door and dropped a cookie sheet atop the stove. Nestled atop the steel sat charred vegetables. What looked like the remains of carrots, potatoes and—were those Brussels sprouts?—were shriveled to the size of small rubber balls and were completely inedible.

He dropped his chin to his chest. "You sure that you don't want to order pizza?"

Chandler pressed her hands to his cheeks and tipped his face to hers. "I love eating chicken all by itself."

He chuckled. "Then chicken we shall have."

* * *

When they were finished eating and the kitchen was cleaned up, Chandler moved to the couch and Hudson followed.

He sat on the opposite end of her and tapped his lap. "Your feet, please."

She smiled, never one to turn down a foot rub. But still…her emotions were whirling inside her.

"What is it?" he asked as if reading her mind.

"Nothing."

"It's something." He patted his lap again, and she slipped off her sandals and slid her feet onto his lap. He pressed his thumbs into the spot just under the ball of each foot, and a moan of pleasure slipped from her lips. "What is it?"

Her eyes, which had been closed, snapped open. "It's nothing."

He dipped his head in a knowing look. "You can tell me. Whatever it is." When she didn't answer, he said, "Is it about the wedding?"

"No. Yes. I don't know." Her hands flew up to her face, and the next thing she knew, Hudson had slid closer to her. He touched her hands and gently pulled them away from her face and pressed them to his heart.

"You can tell me anything, Chand."

She felt his heart beating beneath her hands. There was no way that she could or wanted to keep this from Hudson. He deserved to know the truth, so she grabbed hold of her courage.

She inhaled a deep breath. "It's just that lately, I've been thinking a lot about my dad."

His eyes narrowed. "That's understandable. It's still fresh, what he did to your family."

"I know." The words to tell him the truth jammed up her throat. She couldn't say it, couldn't admit to Hudson, who she'd already put through so much in the past months, the depth of her worry.

When she'd left New York, Chandler had distanced herself from him. She'd lost her muse and was convinced that she wasn't good enough for Hudson or his family. Then he'd come to visit, and she had broken things off completely. Their relationship was over until he showed up one night and said that he wanted to be with her, no matter what.

Now her muse was back, and they were engaged. How could she tell him her next fear?

She would simply have to get over it. That was all there was to it.

"Chand? You in there?"

"Huh?" He was studying her. She blinked. "Sorry. I guess I spaced out."

"I was telling you about my parents." He slid back to his side of the couch and took her feet in his hands, immediately pressing into that same spot beneath the ball of her foot.

"What about them?"

"They're coming for a visit."

"Oh? They are?"

"To see how I'm settling in."

"Ah." Which meant she certainly couldn't tell him her worry now. His parents had already booked plane tickets and were coming.

Maybe her fear would work itself out.

She tipped her head to rest it on the back of the couch and moaned as his fingers dug into a tender spot. "That feels good, and I'm glad they're coming." She lifted her head and forced a smile. "Your parents should get to know my family better and vice versa."

"I couldn't agree more."

"When will they be here?"

"Couple weeks."

"Good. I can't wait to see them." Which was true. His mother was kind, and his father was a caring man. "Do I need to get them a room anywhere?"

"Already taken care of, and there's something else," he started.

"We're having chicken tomorrow night?" she joked.

He flashed her a look that said, *No, we aren't*. It would probably be a while before he ventured to cook them dinner again. But he got huge points for trying.

"I'd like for you to design my wedding band."

His words nearly choked her. She sat up straighter. "You sure?"

"Of course. If I hadn't wanted my proposal to be a surprise, I would've asked you to design your own ring. But that would've defeated the purpose."

"Yes, it would have."

"So?"

She inhaled deeply, knowing that there was only one answer that she could give. "Of course I will. It's the best gift that I could give you."

But even as she said it, Chandler felt her bones sagging. How was she supposed to design rings when her mind was at war with itself?

CHAPTER 12
Ginny

Ginny had come up with the perfect meal for the Teal Scarf Ladies luncheon, which was only a few weeks away. Reece would prepare the Lane Cake and had already put together the West Indies Salad. Everything would be ready in a couple of days, so she picked up her phone to call Mrs. Travis to schedule a time for the tasting.

"Yes, Mrs. Rigby?" Mrs. Travis said when she answered.

She didn't know why, but the old woman made her nervous. Ginny clutched the phone hard as if it would steel her composure. "Good morning, I'm calling to arrange a time for the menu tasting."

"I'll come to you. How's that?"

"Great. We can do the tasting at the café. Does a couple of days from now work?"

"It's fine. I'll see you about two in the afternoon? Will that give you time to finish your lunch service?"

"Yes, it will."

Click. The old woman hung up without saying goodbye, which didn't surprise Ginny in the least. She chuckled to herself and stepped outside to take in the sunshine.

A warm breeze whipped through her hair. Late mornings weren't as hot as they'd been when she'd first arrived in town. Though it was autumn as far as the calendar was concerned, no one had told the beach that yet. It wouldn't truly turn cold until they were well into winter, and that was okay with her. She liked the warmth, though it might make planning her Thanksgiving meal a little different from usual. She couldn't see everyone wanting turkey and heavy cornbread dressing. Perhaps they'd do a simpler menu, something lighter that resembled the local food options.

Which reminded her—she needed to put together a holiday menu for the café. She couldn't exactly ignore Thanksgiving with her customers. Surely Reece would help her come up with the perfect meals for the holiday week.

A truck pulled up and she recognized it as Aiden's. *What was he doing here?* Not that she didn't like seeing him. She did. But they didn't have plans.

She waved and made her way down the old wooden steps as he got out of the truck. The stairs creaked in protest. It was when she was halfway down that she heard a loud *crack*.

Her foot plunged through the wooden step, and Ginny tumbled forward. She threw out her arms, bracing herself for impact. But before she hit the ground, strong arms circled her.

"Steady now," Aiden murmured in her ear as he settled her onto the ground. "You okay?"

Her heartbeat was in her throat, but she was okay. She glanced into his blue eyes and her breath hitched. His salt and fresh pine scent filled her nose, and she wanted to wrap herself up in it.

"Are you okay?"

Was she okay? Why was he asking? Then she realized that he was still holding her. His arms were around her shoulders. One of his hands was clutching her waist, and those eyes...

She swallowed a lump in her throat. "Yes, I'm okay."

His lips were only inches away, but no kiss came. Instead he made sure that she was steady on her feet before letting her go.

He surveyed the stairs, and Ginny watched as his eyes narrowed. "Those need to be replaced."

Her neck felt hot from the closeness with Aiden, and her hand flew to cover it. "I didn't know that they were in such bad shape. They're old, but I didn't realize that the wood was so rotted."

He nodded firmly. "All of them need to be replaced."

"All of them? Do you know someone who can do that?"

He smiled at her. "Me."

She laughed. "You?"

"Yes, me. I can replace them."

"No, no. You don't have to do that."

Aiden shrugged. "I know that I don't have to, but I want to."

Arguing wasn't going to get her anywhere with him. "I'll pay you."

"You won't pay me," he said sternly. "Absolutely not." He took a few steps back. "I'll return in a bit. Don't walk on them before then."

"Where are you going?"

He splayed out his arms and smiled. "To get lumber and my tools."

"I can't talk you out of this, can I?" Did she even want to?

"Nope. I'm already on it."

With that, he hopped into his truck, fired it up and left, leaving Ginny wondering what he had been doing at the café in the first place.

* * *

A couple hours later he was back with lumber, a saw, two sawhorses and a steel box filled that must've housed the rest of his tools.

"That was quick."

He grinned at her, causing warmth to spread across her chest. "I'm efficient."

She laughed. "So it seems. Can I get you anything?"

"No, I'll be fine."

"Well, can I at least help?"

"No, ma'am. I'm going to do this all by myself."

"Okay," she replied with a roll of her eyes. "I'll just be inside if you need me."

"Reading Emma Grace's diary?"

"I wasn't planning on it."

He placed a stair-width piece of wood across the two sawhorses before pulling out his measuring tape. "Well, maybe you should consider it. How else am I ever going to find out what happened to her?"

"I've got other things to do this morning."

"Suit yourself."

Ginny slipped into the house. There was cleaning to do, so she kept herself busy dusting surfaces until Reece came home with an armful of groceries.

"Can I help you?"

"Nah," her daughter said, settling the paper sack on the kitchen counter. "This is it. Hey, what's Aiden doing outside?"

"Fixing our back stairs."

"Why?"

She sighed. "Because one of them broke when I was walking down it."

Panic laced Reece's voice. "Are you okay?"

"Physically I'm fine. Only my pride was wounded." She cocked her head to the bag. "What's all that?"

"This," her daughter said proudly, "is supper—fresh snapper, plus all the ingredients for the Lane cake."

"Is that all we're having? Fish and cake?"

Reece laughed. "Isn't that all we need?"

"For me it is." They both laughed and when it died, Ginny eyed her daughter. She was so pretty and talented. Which reminded her—"Care to tell me about Ted?"

Her back stiffened. "There's nothing to tell."

A faint memory tickled the back of her mind. "Isn't that the guy with the daughter, the one you like?"

"Yep. That's the one. Shelby's got the crush on him."

"Right. Well, what was he doing here?"

"I think he wanted to eat lunch but wound up helping me instead."

"Did you give him anything?"

She grimaced. "No, I didn't."

"Reece—"

"In my defense, he wouldn't take anything."

Ginny crossed her arms as Reece gathered the ingredients to make the cake. "Call and offer him a free lunch. It's the least we can do."

Her shoulders sagged. "What if I don't have his number?"

"Do you?"

"Maybe."

"Then call him. Keep it light. Don't overstep, and you should be fine. But it's the best way to repay him, and he needs to know that we're grateful for his help."

"Fine," she muttered. "I'll do it."

"Good." Ginny stared at her. "Well?"

Her daughter's eyes widened. "You want me to do it right now?"

"Sure I do."

"You're joking."

"Do I look like I'm joking?"

"I'll do it after I bake the cake."

The two women studied one another until Ginny caved. "Fine. Call him later—but do reach out."

"I will," she replied in a prickly voice that made Ginny smile.

Shelby or no Shelby, that man liked Reece. Life was too short for her youngest daughter not to love the man she wanted—if the relationship would ever get that far. Not that she wanted Shelby to get hurt. But if Ted hadn't asked the redhead out yet, that meant he probably wouldn't, which also meant there was a reason for it.

She smiled secretly to herself while Reece worked on the cake. After an hour the comforting smell of vanilla filled the house. If Aiden was still around when it was finished, she'd invite him in for some. Better yet, perhaps he could stay for dinner.

But until then, there was more cleaning to do.

A couple of hours later the back door opened and Aiden walked inside. "All done," he announced.

Ginny's hands flew to her face. She was so embarrassed. She hadn't even checked on him once to see if he needed anything. She had been so busy cleaning and enjoying the smell of the cake, which was done, that she'd lost track of time.

"It's finished?"

"Come see," he told her with a smile.

When she stepped outside, a brand-new stairway with fresh blond wood that smelled like newly cut lumber greeted her.

She covered her mouth in surprise. Ginny couldn't believe that he'd done this for her, and he'd done it simply because she needed it. He hadn't called anyone to do it for him, like Jack would've done. Her previous husband had always been too busy to tackle hands-on issues in their home. Even plumbing emergencies required calling a twenty-four-hour company.

But Aiden...he'd built stairs because it was what was needed.

"Thank you," she whispered, joy flooding her bones. "Thank you so much."

"You're welcome. I'm happy to help, happy to have someone *to help*."

A fissure of energy zapped Ginny all the way to her toes. Her breath caught as she peered into his eyes, and as they fell closer and closer to one another.

This was it. They would kiss here, with the sun sinking in the horizon and while the smell of the ocean mingled with the scent of fresh pine.

Her face tipped up toward his, and their lips were about to touch—

"Mama!"

She jerked back and whipped her head around. Reece stood in the doorway. "You ready for me to put the snapper on?"

"Sure!" She turned to Aiden. "Would you stay for dinner? It's the least I can do to repay you."

He smiled down at her. "I'd love to."

As they walked inside, Ginny's heart ballooned with happiness. The only thing that would've made that moment any more perfect would've been a kiss.

She was beginning to wonder if it would ever happen, or if they would forever be interrupted.

CHAPTER 13
Reece

She stared at the cell phone in her hand, her stomach twisting painfully. Her mother was right, she needed to call and properly thank Ted for his help the other morning. Without him, she would have been lost.

And if she was being honest with herself, which she was, Reece wanted to hear his voice. She felt that he'd been on the very tip of asking her out again that day, but they'd been interrupted by her mother's return.

What harm could it do to call and invite him to have a free lunch? It wouldn't be overstepping any imaginary boundaries. This would be par for the course, right on the correct straight-and-narrow path. She wouldn't be doing anything to betray her friend.

Okay. Deep breath. She could do this.

Reece had his number from when he'd called her before, which seemed like a lifetime ago. Her hand trembled when she hit the call button and lifted the phone to her ear.

Please don't answer. Please don't answer.

"Hello?"

Oh no. He answered. What was she supposed to do now? She couldn't breathe. Her heart was jackhammering against her rib cage. Sweat was sprouting on her forehead.

"Reece?"

"Yes, it's me. Hey. I, um, sorry. I was distracted for a second."

In the background she heard a small voice. "Daddy, can we play now?"

Ted's own voice was low and distant as if he'd pulled the phone from his mouth. "Give me just a minute, sweetheart."

"Then we'll play hide-and-seek?"

A giant hand squeezed Reece's heart until it felt like it would burst. Dear goodness, he was about to play hide-and-seek? He was handsome, kind and a totally doting father?

I cannot fall for him. I cannot fall for him.

"Yeah, honey, give me just a minute," he told Hadley. Reece recalled her name from when Ted had brought his daughter into the restaurant. "Sorry about that," he said, his voice louder now.

"It's fine. I didn't mean to interrupt anything."

"You didn't," he replied, his voice smooth like smoke rolling over velvet. "We hadn't started our hide-and-seek battle for survival yet."

She chuckled. "Okay, well, I'm calling to thank you for what you did the other day?" Why had she made it a question? "When you helped out?" Why was she *still* lifting the end of each sentence? She had to get control of herself. Reece cleared her throat. "Thank you."

"You're most welcome."

Good. One part of the conversation down. "Since I didn't get to properly thank you, I'd like to invite you to have lunch, on us, at the café, whenever you'd like. Feel free to bring Hadley."

"You remember her name," he said, sounding like he was smiling.

"She's so sweet, how could I forget?"

"She liked you a lot."

The conversation was not supposed to go sideways. It had to stay on track. But Reece couldn't stop herself from taking a detour. "She's cute as a button. She really is."

"I appreciate that."

"You're most welcome," she said, repeating his own phrase and allowing, against all her better judgment, for there to be a hint of teasing in her voice.

"Thank you for calling to invite me to lunch, but I can't accept that as payment."

Her stomach fell. "You can't? Why not?"

"Because that's not what I want."

She bristled. "What do you want? An hourly wage?"

He laughed, really barked, then. "No. I don't want money from you. I'd like for you to have dinner with me. That's how you can repay me."

Her stomach twisted in anguish. Oh, goodness. Mayday! Mayday! SOS! This was not how the conversation was supposed to go.

"Well, um…"

"I'm not taking no for an answer."

She scoffed. "Awfully full of yourself, aren't you?"

"I wouldn't say I'm full of myself. I just know when there's something between two people that shouldn't be ignored. Unless you're still seeing that ex-boyfriend of yours."

Her stomach did that falling thing again. Should she lie? She'd already lied to him once, telling him that she had an ex-boyfriend and they were trying to work things out.

The lie sat on the tip of her tongue. It would be easy to let it slip right off, to simply say, *Yes, I'm still seeing my nonexistent ex-boyfriend.* But instead she let the words hang in the air until Ted spoke for her.

"I take it that you're free."

"It's not that simple," she finally managed.

"Then you can explain it to me over dinner. Unless you don't want to go, of course."

It was an out, a perfect out, and Reece should take it. But her heart ached to go out on a date with him, it ached to get to know Ted better, to see that little Hadley again. So as much as she wanted to say no, the words simply wouldn't come out.

In that moment she didn't think of Shelby. Her best friend was absent from her mind as she confessed, "I'd like to go out."

As soon as the words were out in the world, she instantly regretted them. A pang of remorse made her stomach wobble, and as much as she wanted to eat her words, they were gone, slipping into Ted's ears.

"How about Friday night?"

Friday? Friday was good. She didn't have any plans except to apparently stab her best friend in the back. She should tell Ted. She should come clean about Shelby liking him, but for just a moment Reece wanted to feel free. She didn't want to have any responsibilities to anyone but herself.

"Friday is good."

"May I pick you up?"

Her mouth tipped up into a smile. The way he asked, it was so Southern gentleman that her heart swelled. "How about I meet you someplace?"

"Fair enough. Does six sound good? I'll give you details about where to meet when I figure it out."

"Six is perfect."

"Great. See you then."

As soon as they hung up, Reece's insides withered. She'd betrayed her best friend. Shelby would never forgive her.

CHAPTER 14

Shelby

It seemed that everywhere Shelby went, Batton Deats was there. When she headed into Port St. Joe to pick up fresh seafood for her grandmother—Batton was buying some as well. When she needed to grab a present for an old high school friend who'd just had a baby—Batton was strolling down the street right in front of her.

It seemed as if she couldn't throw a rock without hitting her ex squarely in the head.

Worse, every time she saw him, the hurt that he'd caused her flared in her chest, bringing all the pain back. Since this was something she wanted most desperately to avoid, Shelby vowed to stop running into Batton no matter what. So when her grandmother requested that Shelby pick up some groceries, Shelby decided to go farther than Port St. Joe. She headed all the way into Panama City Beach, which was nearly an hour's drive. There was no way on earth that Batton would go there because he hated that tourist trap of a town as much as she did.

So there, she would be safe.

As Shelby scoured the aisles gathering the items from the list that her grandmother had given her, she hummed happily to herself, knowing that this was the last place on earth that she would end up seeing her ex.

As she thought of him, unpleasant memories of what had happened between them ping-ponged in her head.

"Will you marry me?" he had asked her just before high school ended. They'd spent the day at the beach and had gone back to her house to clean up. Somehow he'd kept a ring with him the entire day, managing to keep it free from sand, so it was sparkling by the time he got down on one knee and proposed.

She'd said yes, of course, throwing her arms around his neck. The joy that filled her in that moment broke her heart in two as she replayed the memory in her head.

They'd been happy—*blissfully happy*—until everything fell apart. There were several weeks of school left, and he was on the baseball team. They'd gone away, traveling for a game. When he returned, Batton had told her that they should end things. That it was for the best.

It was so unexpected. Where had this come from, she had asked. He replied that it was the way things should go. He was sorry that they wouldn't work out.

Didn't he love her? She had begged him to answer, but he never replied.

Shelby had been devastated. How could he end things before they even began? She told him that she never wanted to see him again. Then she mailed the ring back to him and worked diligently to avoid him in school, making sure to take different paths to her classes and eating lunch where he wouldn't find her. She was a senior anyway and didn't have many classes left, so she could go to school late and leave early. It was easier to avoid Batton than she'd ever imagined.

Eventually he left, heading off to college and apparently becoming an architect. He probably had a beautiful girlfriend now and was calling her every day while he was here. Well, she would show him. Or maybe she wouldn't since Shelby had decided not to care. Batton Deats would not take up any more real estate in her brain.

That was the exact thought going through her head when she rounded the corner of an aisle and crashed her cart into another one headfirst.

"I'm sorry," she said, her eyes flaring from the jolt of the minor collision.

"My fault," came the reply in a voice that was impossible for her not to recognize.

"Batton?" she snapped, glaring into his blue eyes.

"Shelby?" he replied, sounding just as disgusted as her.

That was it. Was he following her? "Are you stalking me?"

"Stalking you?" His eyes narrowed to slitty wedges of death. "Why would I be stalking you?"

"That's exactly what I want to know. But everywhere I go, there you are. I specifically came here because I know you hate this city."

His eyes flared with anger. "Everywhere *you* go? Everywhere *I* go, there *you* are. I can't get away from you. I knew our town was small, but I didn't expect it to be so small that I'd run into you every five seconds. Believe me, I don't want to see you any more than you want to see me."

"Fine."

"Good."

"Now get out of my way," she commanded.

"Happily."

They reversed their carts and headed in opposite directions. She went down the pasta aisle and he went down…a different aisle that she was too angry to remember what it stocked.

She was minding her own business picking out spaghetti sauce when a cart stopped beside her.

"I need some spaghetti sauce," he said.

Oh. My. Gosh. Was he really beside her, asking her to move?

Shelby tipped her head and glared at him. "I was here first."

"Then hurry up and pick one."

"There's a specific one my grandmother likes."

"The one without sugar." He reached over her, plucked it from the shelf and handed it over.

Shelby hesitated before taking it. When she did, her fingers brushed his, and a spark ignited her body. There was not supposed to be electricity between them. Shame on her bad body for betraying her like that.

"And if you want the pasta she likes, it's over there," he told her.

Her gaze tracked to where his finger was pointing, and sure enough, there was the brand and cut of pasta that she always got for her grandmother.

"You remember," she whispered, a lump in her throat.

"Yeah."

A thick silence blanketed them, and Shelby dared to look at him. His gaze was trained on her, those blue eyes searching hers in a way that made her breath hitch.

The desire to reach out and touch him pulsed through her veins, but she didn't know anything about him now—not his life, not what he liked or didn't like. But still, it seemed rude to just take the pasta and go, so she cleared her throat.

"How's your dad?"

"He's okay. Taking it easy, so I'm helping around the house."

"Still working at the hobby shop?"

He rolled his eyes. "You make it sound like that's what I do for a living. No. It was a one-day thing."

"I see." What a terrible reply, but she didn't know what else to say. "Well, I'll be seeing you around."

But she didn't move and neither did he. They continued to stare at one another as if daring the other to speak first.

"You know," he said, a lopsided grin on his face, "you look exactly the same as you did in high school."

"Is that a compliment?"

"I think so."

She exhaled a shaky breath. Why was she nervous? She should be angry. "Then thank you."

She pushed the cart forward, and his voice stopped her again. "How's Vera?"

"She's good." Then she added, "Slowing down, as comes with age."

"Same thing happened to my grandpa. It's hard watching them slow down."

"Yeah."

"How's the gas station?"

She cocked a brow and studied him skeptically. "It's good. How'd you know we're still running it?"

His hand flew to the back of his neck, and he rubbed, looking bashful all of a sudden. "I just…heard."

"Ah." It seemed impolite to not ask about him, so she managed, "How's architecting?"

He chuckled. "Is that a word?"

"It is now," she replied, folding her arms.

"It's good. Better than I ever hoped." His blue eyes shone on her, and Shelby remembered what it was like to be in Batton's gaze. His eyes were a spotlight, and she was the star. "I've been offered partner at the firm."

"Partner? Impressive. I'm sure you worked hard for that offer."

"Harder than I would have liked."

"What do you mean?" Shelby genuinely wanted to know, which both annoyed and surprised her.

A woman with three kids trailing behind her came up behind Shelby, and she pushed her cart on with Batton walking steadily beside her. There was barely room for both carts side by side, but he stayed with her, never bumping into a thing.

"Well," he said in answer to her question, "making partner means making sacrifices."

"Long hours?"

"Not just that, but it really puts a toll on your personal life. It's hard to be a regular person when you're working eighty hours a week."

"As an architect?"

"Don't sound so surprised," he said with a laugh. "It's a competitive business."

"But you love it?"

"Yes. I do. I wouldn't trade it for anything else…but I'm not sure I want to be partner. Being here, seeing my dad…I don't know."

Batton had a heart after all. But even though she tried to steel herself against him, she couldn't help but soften at the care in his voice.

Yet she didn't soften too much. She was supposed to hate him, wasn't she?

"How about you?" he said, expertly changing the subject.

"What about me?"

"The gas station. Are you happy there?"

They came to the end of the aisle, and Shelby took a right, expecting Batton to break away, but instead he stuck to her side. She wasn't sure if she was annoyed or happy for his presence.

"Happy at the gas station? I don't know. It's the family business and Nana loves it."

"Not your passion. It never was."

Her heart cracked in two that he remembered. She expected him to ask why she never left. That would've given her the chance to say, *We were supposed to leave together. I couldn't go without you.*

"And you never left," he added quietly.

She expected to bristle, but when it came right down to it, her anger didn't flare like expected. "I stayed. I like Sugar Cove, and my grandmother needed me."

"Like my family does now." He sounded sad. "Eventually we're all needed. I guess it just matters on whether or not we embrace that task or if we pawn it off on someone else."

"I guess so." She glanced over at him. Batton was looking straight ahead, but when she glanced over, his face tipped toward her. Her stomach flip-flopped and she ripped her gaze away, staring ahead as she turned down another aisle, him still beside her. "But you're going back, right? You have to return because of the whole partner thing."

"Yeah, I have to go back. I can't stay gone forever. I'm burning up vacation days as it is coming here."

"How much vacation do you have?"

"Three months."

She nearly choked on literally nothing. "Three months?"

He rubbed the back of his neck again, a gesture she recalled that he only did when feeling embarrassed. "Like I said, trying to make partner requires a lot of sacrifice; taking vacations is one of them. But I'm still working, drawing plans, and calling clients while I'm here."

"So, it's not really a vacation," she teased.

"With my dad the way he is, it wouldn't be anyway."

The sorrow in his voice nearly broke her heart. But as the first hint of the icy muscle melting, she steeled herself, and the depth of his betrayal rushed through her body like a tidal wave.

She grabbed the last item on her list. "That's it for me. I'm going to check out now. It was..." Good catching up? Great to see him? She wasn't ready to go there. "Have a nice day."

As she turned to enter the checkout line, his voice stopped her once again. "Shelby?"

Her knees quaked. She'd forgotten how the sound of her name on his lips made her weak. She cleared her throat in a poor attempt to erase thoughts of him.

"Yes?"

"Would you...like to grab coffee sometime?"

Her fingers curled tighter around the bar of the shopping cart. Her mind screamed, *Yes! Do it!* But the frost crusting her heart said otherwise.

"No, I don't think so," she replied as she kept right on walking, straight into the open checkout line.

CHAPTER 15
Ginny

"We haven't spoken in weeks. You've got to tell me everything that's going on," Farrah demanded.

She couldn't help but laugh at her best friend. "Are you being nosy because you miss me or because you want to live vicariously through me?"

"You know me too well, Ginny Rigby. Now dish, or else I'll drive down there today, and we'll be having supper on the beach."

"Promise?" Her chest tightened at how much she missed her best friend. "A beachside dinner sounds wonderful."

"Would if I could, but I've got…things going on here."

"Oh? Care to talk about it?"

"After you tell me everything. Now, what's going on with that hunky man you've been seeing?"

She settled back onto a pillow and laughed. It was early in the morning, and she'd just made herself a cup of tea and had come back to her bed for some well-deserved reading time. She'd only just cracked the spine of her newest paperback when Farrah called.

"Hunky man?" she repeated innocently.

"Don't you try to get out of this. I want to know everything about him."

"He took me on a picnic to a deserted island not far away."

"He didn't! The man must be crazy about you. Sounds so romantic. Did y'all kiss?"

It felt like they were teenagers, gossiping about cute boys. "No, we were interrupted by toxic-waste-sized bees."

"What?" Farrah shrieked.

"Let's just say no one was hurt, but there was no kissing."

"Darn." Her voice dropped like a stone falling off a cliff. "What else?"

"He made me a new set of steps leading down from the back of the lighthouse."

"Did you ask him to?"

"No."

There was a loud exhalation from Farrah. "Oh my gosh, he's in love. And he can do manly things—maneuver a boat, build stairs. What else can he do? If he's this good with his hands already, it makes me wonder."

Heat crept up her cheeks. "Stop it. We only just started seeing one another. Besides, I'm not ready for anything more."

"I understand. You have every right to want to take things slow. You've been through the ringer. But all I'm saying is that you deserve to have a little fun with someone who really seems into you, and speaking of ghosts from the past—"

"Were we speaking about Jack?" she asked as she glanced out the window. The sun was already high in the sky, as it was when you lived at the beach. There was no hiding from the sun, no mountain peaks to shield you from its rays. "I didn't think you'd even mentioned his name."

"I hadn't, but from what I hear, *that woman* is having a heck of a time with the society ladies."

It felt like her chest was being squeezed between two brick walls. The mention of *that woman's* name always caused her body to react on its own. Even though she didn't want to talk about her, Farrah had brought up the subject for a reason.

"What do you mean, she's having a problem?"

Her voice became louder, as if she was pressing her mouth to the receiver. "From what I understand, she got her child enrolled in school and has tried doing things with the PTO. The other mothers are letting her, but word's gotten out about who she is—you know, from the grandmothers—and no one talks to her. She's already a social pariah, and she just moved in. No one wants to have anything to do with the woman." Farrah scoffed. "What does she expect? You can't take over a person's house and life and expect everyone to welcome you with open arms, not when you were the mistress."

"She called me."

"What?" Farrah screeched. "No!"

"What did she say?"

"I have no idea. I didn't answer."

Her friend scoffed. "I don't blame you. Why would you want to talk to her? The nerve, calling you." She was quiet for a moment before saying, "Maybe she wanted to apologize. Maybe she wanted to offer your old house back. Ginny! What if that's it? What if *that woman* was calling to say that it wasn't working out in Atlanta, and she wanted to hand over the house. You could come back to your old life. We could be together. You could help me…"

When her voice died, Ginny frowned. It wasn't like Farrah to be quiet. Silence was not her strong suit. "I could help you what? What were you going to say?"

"Nothing. It's nothing."

"Farrah," she warned, "I know you better than anyone else on this earth. Something is bothering you. What is it?" When her friend was still quiet, she persisted. "You were there for me when my life imploded. Let me help you. Not that your life is going sideways like mine did," she added with a weak laugh, because worry was knotting her chest. Farrah was loud and open, her thoughts barely touching her head before they exploded from her mouth. But now she was quiet, and that worried Ginny.

"It's just that I'm afraid that…well that…I don't know how to say this."

"I'm your oldest friend in the world. You can tell me anything."

She released a staggering breath. "I'm afraid that Evan is…it just seems like he might be…"

"Cheating?"

"Yes." The word came out in a rush, as if she'd been holding on to it for way too long before finally deciding to release it. "I hate to think that, but he's been acting so strange lately. He's started working out really hard and is spending more time away from home."

It certainly did sound suspicious. However, there was a time and a place for jumping to conclusions. "I'm certainly not an expert at smelling this sort of thing out. I didn't even know Jack had a second family. But I can say that Evan loves you."

"This is different, Ginny. It feels different. I don't know."

It felt like her bones were being crushed under the weight of listening to Farrah. The last thing that she wanted was for her friend to be hurting. "Maybe it's a big misunderstanding."

"Maybe," she said softly.

"But you don't have any proof."

"No, I don't."

"Until you have proof, there's nothing to talk about, is there? Farrah, you can jump to conclusions as much as you want, and you can speculate, but that will only drive you crazy. It'll also drive a wedge between you and Evan. If you don't trust him, the relationship isn't going to work. You've been married long enough to know that. For me it's different. If I had known about Jack, then I would've done something. But you only suspect Evan."

"Maybe I should hire a private investigator," she joked bitterly.

"Evan is a good man," she told her friend in a soothing voice. "He loves his family and God. He's active in the church and lives the straight and narrow life. If he's working out, maybe it's because he either wants to get in shape or he wants to impress you."

"Maybe," Farrah replied, but it was obvious that she didn't believe what she was saying.

"You should ask him."

She snorted. "It's not like he'll admit anything. If he's cheating, he won't say, 'Yes, I'm cheating, Farrah.'"

"You're right, but will it make you feel better? Will it help ease the worry in your mind? You're my best friend, and I know this is bothering you."

"Mm. But that's enough about me. Are you going to call *that woman* back?"

Ever since Jack's mistress had taken over her life, they had taken to referring to her as *that woman* rather than saying her name.

"Why should I call her? What could she possibly want?"

"Maybe she wants to give you some of your furniture."

It was Ginny's turn to scoff. "I doubt it. She's waited this long to reach out. I'm sure she's grabbed all our things for herself."

"What about the pictures? What about Reece's things? She hadn't completely cleaned out her room, right?"

"That's true." She scraped her teeth over her bottom lip. "Reece hasn't mentioned it in a while, but there were some things that she wanted to get."

"Have them shipped," Farrah quipped. "Let them be sent right to you. Don't ever go back there."

She chuckled at the severity in her friend's voice. "You have a point. Well, then. Maybe I'll call her back."

"Just don't invite her to Thanksgiving dinner."

She sucked air. "It's coming up soon."

"Do y'all want to come up here? You know the city is so pretty during the holidays."

Ginny loved the city that time of year—so many lights and events to attend. Though it was tempting to leave, she needed to get used to her new life. "We'll stay here, in Sugar Cove. But you're welcome to visit."

"I might. I may end up leaving my husband for all we know."

"Farrah," she said quietly. "You need to talk to Evan before you do anything rash."

"I will."

"Promise?"

"Cross my heart."

They hung up, promising to check in with each other in a few days. But as Ginny got off the phone, she couldn't help but wonder if Farrah's promise would hold up or if she would risk ruining a solid twenty-year marriage.

Either way, only time would tell.

CHAPTER 16

Emma Grace

Diary, I've been so terrible. I want to say that I've been a good, mindful young woman, but that isn't true.

I've been meeting Jim in secret, walking into town when Papa's at home. We meet for ice cream, to have a soda at the pharmacy, to watch a matinee on Saturday. He is so kind, Diary.

Last Saturday we met at the theater, and he brought me a rose. A rose! I've never been given anything like that before.

His cheeks were red as he handed it to me, almost the same color as the petals.

"Thank you," I told him. "It's beautiful."

"Not as beautiful as you."

The smile that came afterward was so big that it made my cheeks hurt. My heart swelled, too. I always thought that wasn't true, that your heart couldn't swell from happiness, but now I know that it is. Your heart can get so big that it feels like it's going to break through your ribs.

That's how happy being with Jim has made me. So happy, Diary. In fact, we have a secret date tonight. He's taking me to a fair that's come to town. I've told Papa that I'm going with some girls, and so he doesn't mind, as long as I'm back before it gets too late. He never knows when the lamp might go out and he'll have to change the light. It's a two-person *job, and it would be just our luck that a bunch of ships would be in the ocean the one night we have to change the light.*

Most of the time no ships are out late. I don't suspect trouble, but I will be back at a good hour for Papa so that he doesn't worry.

Or become suspicious.

* * *

The fair was everything that I thought it would be. Clowns were sprinkled throughout the grounds juggling bowling pins or unicycling through the crowds.

I tried cotton candy! Papa frowns upon sweets, so when Jim saw a man twirling a stick and gathering what looked like pink spiderwebs on it, he said, "Let me buy you cotton candy."

Butterflies took flight in my chest, Diary. I must've had eyes as big as plates because he laughed, tipping his head as if he wanted to get a better look at me. His eyes are so green—and flecked with gold. They're gorgeous.

But anyway, he laughed kindly. "Haven't you ever tried cotton candy before?"

"No," I admitted, feeling like a girl who never left the family farm except for church on Sundays.

He threaded his fingers through mine. "Then I'll buy you some."

"But you've already paid for my ticket."

He jerked his chin to the man behind the candy stand. "And does that mean I can't buy you anything else? Are you going to tell me what I can spend my money on?"

His words were firm, but his tone was joking, so I smiled. "I won't tell you what to spend one penny on. If you want to buy me a big teddy bear, then go ahead."

He threw his head back and laughed. "How about we start with the candy?"

"I'll take it."

It was magical to watch the man twirl the stick and see the thin strands of sugar wrap around it. It didn't look like much at first, but after a minute, the man had a whole pink cloud wrapped around that stick. He handed it to me with a smile and Jim paid.

Eating the candy was like biting into a sugary cloud that melted into crystals as soon as it touched my tongue. My eyes must've shown it, too, because Jim laughed.

"Looks like it's good."

"It's so good." I held the stick out to him, and he leaned over, taking a bite but watching me the whole time. He tucked a strand of hair behind my ears, and where he touched me, I could feel the heat of his fingers making a blazing line on my skin.

"Delicious," he declared before tugging me toward the Tunnel of Love.

"What's that?"

"A ride. It's in the dark. If you don't want to go, I understand."

I didn't want to look like a chicken. I wanted to be smart and older. "Let's go on it."

We got in a small boat that was pushed off by a man with an oar. The water wasn't deep. I leaned over to look, and Jim laughed.

"Are you looking for fish?"

"I was thinking about it."

"When I leave this place, I don't want to have anything to do with fish."

"You don't like the ocean?"

He shook his head just before darkness closed up around us. "All I do is fish, Emma. My father's livelihood is based on the whims of the ocean, whether it wants to give us fish one day or keep them all to itself the next. No. I want more." He nudged my arm. "What about you? What do you want?"

We were in complete darkness now. It was a big question. For all my life I'd been with Papa and couldn't see myself leaving him. But Jim was a flame, and though I wasn't a moth that wanted to burn up, I wanted to be near him. For the first time in all my life, I didn't want to be tied to a place where I had to man a light every night, often working on very little sleep. I wanted something else, too.

Freedom, I realized. I wanted freedom, to be out in the world and to be more than what I was, to see more than what I had already. To live in a city, where there were honking cars and people moving quickly. When your life revolved around the ocean, you had to stay near it, never going too far inland.

I understood exactly what Jim was saying, the ache that he felt in his chest for more. I felt it, too, and more than that, I understood it. I understood him.

"You want to get out too, don't you?" he whispered, his face close to mine. I could feel his breath blowing against my cheeks. He smelled of cotton candy.

"Yes," I admitted. Just saying the word made it feel like my chest was cracking open, releasing a stone that had been stuffed inside of it. "I don't want to be in a lighthouse anymore."

I heard him swallow. I couldn't see a thing in the pitch-black, not even my hand.

"Then I'll get us both out," he told me.

I laughed nervously. "What?"

He took my hand, and it felt like a line of lightning shimmied up my arm. "Just what I said. We'll leave—together. Find a way out of here."

"Jim, I..."

"I'm not saying we'll go tomorrow. But if I leave, will you come with me?"

I hesitated. He was asking me to go with him unmarried. No one did that.

"Don't worry," he said. "It'll be proper."

I sighed. "Oh."

"You don't have to answer now."

Which was good because my mind was swirling. Jim was asking me to leave. He wanted me to go with him, to leave my father, to leave this life.

A faint light glowed up ahead.

"Emma?" he said, his face still angled toward mine. His breath caressed my cheeks. Jim released my hand, and then both of his cradled my face. The pads of his rough fingers took me gently, tipping me toward him.

"Yes?" I said, breathless. My heart was beating a thousand times a minute. *My head was clouded over. Not one actual thought was in my brain. All I could focus on was the feel of his calloused fingers on my skin, how close our mouths were, and then...*

His lips gently covered mine. Diary, I'd never been kissed before. I'd seen plenty of kisses in the movies, but I when it came to actually doing the deed, I wasn't sure what to do, how to move my mouth.

But it didn't matter, because Jim's lips moved, and I moved with them. It felt like every bone in my body was melting. I was certain to become a puddle in the bottom of the boat. I closed my eyes and focused on his soft yet firm lips.

That must have been what heaven felt like.

Light started pricking my eyes. We were out of the tunnel. But before I could break away, a voice shouted, "Emma!"

My eyes popped open as a hand roughly took me by the arm and yanked me out of the boat.

Papa stood before me. His face was gaunt, his beard scruffier than I remembered it being that morning. Fury blazed in his dark eyes, and he snarled, "Haven't I taught you better than this, girl?"

"Sir," Jim said, climbing from the boat. Oh Diary, you should've seen the fear on his face. I'd never known Jim to ever be scared, but I could tell right then and there that he was afraid. But I couldn't tell you what he was afraid of, exactly.

As quickly as I realized the fear in his eyes, my father cut him off. "And you—stay away from my daughter. Don't ever come near her."

"Sir, you don't even know who I am."

"I know who you are," Papa spat, his hand still curled around my arm so tightly I winced. "And I know your no-good father. Keep away from my daughter or else you'll regret it."

Without another word Papa dragged me away so roughly that I lost my grip on the stick of cotton candy. It fell to the grass and was trampled by strangers within seconds. I twisted to look back at Jim, and he stared at me longingly.

He looked as helpless and shameful as I did, and I couldn't help but to think that my heart had been trampled just like that cotton candy.

CHAPTER 17
Chandler

Chandler stared at the band of yellow gold that she'd just pulled from the mold and polished it with a cloth. The band gleamed under the lights, the surface as reflective as a pond.

She studied it and sighed. It was beautiful, perfect, and would do nicely for Hudson's wedding band. But it wasn't right. A pit opened in her stomach. There wasn't a rational explanation for why the ring wasn't the right one, but it just wasn't. She spotted the trash and was tempted to toss it in.

"What have you got there?" Vicki asked.

She looked over her shoulder and spotted the store owner standing in the doorway. A silk cardigan spanning the color range of peacock feathers was draped over her shoulders.

"It's supposed to be Hudson's wedding band."

Vicki perched her jade reading glasses atop her nose. "May I see?"

"Sure."

She rose and passed the ring over, then she rubbed at her neck, getting the knots and cramps from it. The smell of coffee wafted into the room, which meant that Vicki had been making her favorite blend —an autumnal offering sweetened with maple syrup.

"The coffee smells good."

Vicki flashed her a grin. "It's my favorite. Even if it doesn't get cold here until well after autumn, that's not going to stop me from enjoying everything that reminds me of it—pumpkin lattes included."

She laughed, understanding the woman's love for fall food offerings because Chandler loved them herself. Thinking of it made her miss New York—the crisp fall air, the leaves turning in Central Park, eating hot candied peanuts from a food vendor—they were all such good memories.

"It's a beautiful band," Vicki murmured before handing it back.

"Thanks."

"But you don't like it."

"I don't know. It just doesn't seem right." She dragged the polishing cloth off the table and ran it over the surface again. "But thank you."

"Wait here."

Vicki left the room, and Chandler slipped the band into a velvet box. When the store owner returned, she was holding two steaming mugs of coffee.

"Here."

She eagerly took the warm mug. Heat from the ceramic seeped into her hands, into her bones, even, warming her all the way to her toes. She took a tiny sip and smiled. Coffee mixed with maple syrup was sheer bliss.

"It's good?" Vicki asked.

"It's perfect."

"Want milk?"

She shook her head. "No. I like it just the way it is."

"Now, sit."

Chandler did so, taking the chair at the worktable. Vicki sat in the recliner that was stationed on the other side of the studio. Lining the walls between them sat shelves stuffed to bursting with books on jewelry making and small tubs filled with stones and metal. There was also an antique oak hutch pushed up against the wall. It was filled with the tools of the trade, and potted ferns and a crimson oriental rug lined the floor.

Vicki always said that even though a studio was a workspace, it needed to welcome the muse of creativity, so the space needed to be beautiful as well as functional.

Chandler agreed.

From where she sat on the recliner, the goldsmith cleared her throat. "I hope the other day, when we spoke, that I didn't say anything out of bounds—when I brought up your father, that is."

"Oh, no."

Her gaze dropped to the mug she cradled in her lap. "I know that it's been hard on your family, what he did, and I hope that my words didn't affect your engagement."

It felt like a spear had penetrated her heart. Her throat closed when she replied, "No, not at all."

Vicki's gaze very purposefully (or so it seemed to her) dragged from Chandler to the ring and back. "There's nothing wrong with that band."

"It just isn't right for Hudson."

"Make another one."

She'd already made two others; both engraved all the way around. But they hadn't been right either, so that was how the plain band had come into being.

She sighed and told Vicki about the ones already made.

The studio owner studied her. "I know that I've told you a bit about my old love."

"You have."

"How I wished that we'd worked harder to stay together."

"Right."

"And that's true. If he'd asked me to marry him, I don't know what I would have said. I like to think that my answer would have been yes, but I was pursuing a career, and that career came first. But if he had asked me, I wouldn't have entered the relationship dooming it to failure before it even started. I apologize if what I said the other day made you doubt Hudson. I've met him, and I don't question his love for you, not in the least. He moved here for you, Chandler. Only a man in love does such a thing."

"Right. I know."

Vicki cocked her chin. "But what?"

She shook her head. "Nothing. There is no but."

"Are you sure?"

Here it was, an invitation to spill her guts, to release every ounce of doubt that pricked her mind over and over. But turning those doubts into words seemed shallow after all that Hudson had done for her. It would sound like she was looking for an excuse *not* to marry him, and that wasn't it. She wanted an excuse *to* marry him if anything. She wanted to be Chandler Wheeler.

It was just that her father's actions had now stained what love would forever be to her. No matter who was asking for her hand, Chandler was worried that there would always be a seed of doubt in her mind, that she would struggle with trust.

It had been so easy for her father to simply have a second family, to pretend that everything was fine. If it had been easy for Jack Rigby, didn't that mean it would be easy for anyone else?

"Life is so short, Chandler," Vicki continued. "Don't let fear stop you from reaping the benefits of it, like I let ambition get the best of me. I've never met another man that I loved, not like my first love, and I doubt that I ever will again."

And she loved Hudson, that was the thing. He set her soul on fire when he looked at her, skimmed his fingers down her arm, even quirked his lips into a smile. Just thinking of him made her stomach flip-flop. But dread pooled in her stomach at the same time, that little voice in the back of her head chiming that she could wind up like her mother—abandoned and humiliated.

"Just let me know if there's anything you want to talk about." Vicki's gaze flicked to the ring on the table behind her. "And if you decide that isn't right for Hudson, you can always sell it here. It's beautiful and will be snatched up in a second. Men like wide bands like it."

She did, too. But that didn't stop her stomach from plummeting at the thought of slipping it on his finger.

"When are his parents coming?" Vicki asked.

"Sorry?" Oh, right. She'd mentioned that they'd be visiting and that she'd likely be out of the studio while they were in Sugar Cove. "In a few days."

"Before Thanksgiving, huh?"

"They do a big Thanksgiving dinner back in New York."

"Are you going to it?"

Was she? Hudson hadn't said anything about it. "Oh, um, no, I'm staying here with my mama. It's her first holiday at the lighthouse."

Vicki smiled. "Then I'm sure it'll be special."

"Yes, it will be."

Which got her to thinking about Thanksgiving. What were Hudson's plans?

* * *

"What are you doing for Thanksgiving?" Chandler asked later while Hudson was grilling chicken outside, on the small smoker he'd purchased from the hardware store in town. "Your parents are coming here before then, but we haven't discussed the holiday."

He flipped the chicken and lowered the lid. "My mom asked me to come home." He slid past her, trailing his finger along her waist as he reached around with his other hand to grab his beer from the table and take a pull. "Why?"

She stiffened. "We just haven't talked about it, is all."

He settled the beer down and swiped the back of his hand across his lips, erasing the drops of beer clinging to his upper lip.

"That's because I knew you'd want to stay here, with your mom, and since this is likely my last Thanksgiving as a single man, I thought it would be best to go home. Once we're married, things will be different."

She folded her arms. "What do you mean?"

He slumped onto a chair and pulled her to sit atop him. He placed one hand on her hip, and with the other he smoothed her hair over one shoulder. "Well, for starters, we'll be doing everything together, so next year we may decide to stay here or go to New York. We'll have to toggle it, and once we have kids, there'll be even more to juggle."

His hand caressed her back, making lazy circles over her shirt. Her mind went slack the same as her spine as she rolled his words around in her head—kids, trips, juggling.

Then she snapped out of it. "You're going to New York by yourself and didn't tell me."

"Time to check the chicken." He eased her off his lap and slid around her. When he opened the smoker's lid, a thick wall of gray smoke rolled out, vanishing Hudson's head for half a second before a wind flicked it away. He turned the chicken and nodded in approval. "Only a few more minutes."

"New York," she reminded him testily.

"Right. I didn't think it was a big deal. I haven't seen my family since moving here, and I didn't think you'd care." He turned to her and placed both hands on her waist, pivoting her to face him. "But if you don't want me to go, I'll stay. We can watch the parade on TV, eat macaroons—whatever you want."

She laughed. "Eat macaroons? Where did that come from?"

"It just came to me. Don't say us lawyers can't be creative." He pressed his forehead to hers, leaving an imprint of heat on her flesh. "It doesn't matter what I do. If you want me to stay, I'll stay."

"You already booked your ticket, didn't you?"

"Busted."

"I should be very annoyed that you didn't tell me."

He brushed his lips over her forehead. "You're welcome to be. I should've said something earlier, but I knew you'd need to stay here."

She tugged on the lapels of his short-sleeved linen shirt. "You guessed right. If you want to go, it's okay."

He leaned back and smiled that gorgeous, sunlight-breaking-through-storm-clouds smile of his. "My mom will try to talk you into coming, too."

"Will she?"

"I'm sure."

He kissed her and Chandler's heart softened. He would be gone for a couple of days. This might be good. It would be a good test for her. If she could trust him for a few days, then she could see how she'd fare when they married.

Perhaps Hudson leaving for Thanksgiving was a blessing. Yes, it was, she decided, and that was how she'd look at it.

When they parted, she locked her arms around his neck and

grinned up at him. As they stared into each other's eyes, the scent of charred meat wafted up her nose. "What is that? Is something burning?"

"The chicken!"

Hudson broke away and spun to the cooker. He lifted the lid and waved away the wall of smoke. He grabbed the thongs and quickly turned the breasts, which were covered in thick scorched bands. His shoulders fell.

"Burnt chicken—again."

She came up beside him and said in a cheerful voice, "We'll just scrape that side off."

He tipped his chin down, and one side of his mouth ticked up. His brown eyes overflowed with warmth. "One day I'm going to cook chicken for you that doesn't burn."

She threw her head back and laughed. "I can't wait to eat it."

CHAPTER 18

Reece

Sweat coated Reece's palms and her hair was plastered to the back of her neck, glued there with even more perspiration. She fidgeted with the neck of her dress while standing outside the door of Southern Patio, the restaurant that Ted had suggested they eat at.

She glanced up at the porch. The place was grandiose, to say the least. It was a huge white building that was both tall and wide. From what she had heard, the restaurant seconded as an event venue specializing in weddings, so the scope of it made sense.

She exhaled a heavy breath. Reece had worn a new white halter dress that she'd bought. It had a flowing skirt that just brushed her knees, and it cinched tight at the waist, showing off her figure. She'd slimmed down since arriving at the lighthouse. Being on her feet half the day had a way of working out the calories that she consumed from eating the baked goods that she made.

Her hair was piled high atop her head, and the wedged espadrilles on her feet gave height that her petite frame normally lacked.

She'd only been standing by the front door for a few minutes when she heard Ted's voice. "Sorry for being late."

She glanced at her watch. "You're not late."

He smiled, revealing a dimple in his left cheek. "I know, but you're early, and I wanted to beat you. If Hadley hadn't foiled my plan by refusing to let me leave, I would've done so."

Reece's heart slammed against her ribs at the image of the little girl crying for her father. "Was she okay when you left?"

"She was fine. My mother got her calmed down. All it takes is a story and that girl's just fine."

He stepped close and the scent of his cologne trickled up her nose—leather and sandalwood. She stopped herself from pressing her nose into his shirt and drinking up the smell because it was literally the best scent she'd ever inhaled—and that was saying a lot since she loved the smell of warm yeast mingled with cinnamon.

"How're you?" he asked.

His sandy hair looked like he'd run his fingers through it and that was all. It was fairly windblown, and his blue eyes sparkled when he smiled, showing that dimple again.

Maybe it was his smile, maybe it was his smell, but either way Reece felt like she was being pulled toward him, as if Ted had his own gravity and she was an asteroid with no other choice but to be sucked in.

To keep herself from falling, she focused on his clothes. He wore a camel-colored suit jacket and a blue shirt with no tie. He looked nice. This place looked nice. Too nice.

"And I thought you were just going to take me out for pizza," she teased.

"I've probably got leftover pizza in the seats of my SUV if you'd like to check. Hadley has a way of storing food for winter."

She laughed. "All good kids do."

He nodded toward the front door. "Would you like to go in?"

No, she wouldn't. If they went inside, that meant she was breaking a promise to her friend. If they stayed out here, in the humid air, then she wouldn't be betraying Shelby.

"Um."

He took another step, and the warm glow of lights from the restaurant fell over his face, which only made her heart beat faster.

"This is about Shelby, isn't it?"

A knot formed in her throat. "What?" Why was she saying, *what?* Why didn't she just say, *Yes! I can't betray my best friend, but you smell really good, and I want to bury my face in your shirt.*

Well, that was clearly inappropriate.

"Look, I know that she likes me, and that you're her friend. And I suspect that from the start the reason you wouldn't go out with me was because of her."

"Um…" She was obviously still losing the conversation battle. "Well…"

That was no better than her first try, but it didn't need to be because Ted continued. "I've known Shelby a long time. We're friends, and that's all we'll ever be. I've never had a reason to tell her that because it's never come up. On second thought, I've never had a reason to tell her *until now.*"

She couldn't breathe. Somewhere between him saying that he knew Shelby liked him and never needing to tell her, her lungs had stopped working. Oh, wait. There they went. She took a deep inhale.

"I, uh…"

"You don't have to say anything. I know you wouldn't betray her trust, but I also know you're here." He took a step closer, and the heat of his body wafted onto her, sinking into her flesh and making chill bumps crawl down her spine. "So why don't we go have dinner and not worry about anything else?" His gaze dropped from her eyes to take in the dress. He didn't look at her with desire or want, simply with appreciation. "You look stunning, by the way."

"I was going for sea-breeze casual."

He laughed then, *really* laughed, from his belly, and it sounded like home to her. It made her skin ripple, and the flip-flopping in her stomach halted.

When he stopped laughing, his eyes sparkled as he smiled. "Are you hungry?"

"Very."

"Then let's eat."

* * *

"So, you grew up here," she asked, picking at the grilled shrimp appetizer that she had decided on for dinner. Ted had opted for the pork chop, which looked so good that she had been tempted to steal a bite.

"In Sugar Cove, yes," he told her. "And what made y'all move here?"

Reece didn't want to go there, not on a first date. "My mom needed a change. Turned out we all did."

"That's right." He took a bite of pork chop and moaned. "You sure you don't want some?"

"No thanks."

"It's delicious," he told her, waving around a piece that was stuck to his fork. "You're missing out."

"Sure. Okay."

"I knew you were dying for a bite. You've been eyeing my plate ever since it arrived."

She smiled and speared the bite he pushed onto her plate with her fork. The meat practically melted when it hit her tongue.

"Oh, wow. That is good."

"See? I told you." Their gazes collided, and Reece found herself falling again. He must've felt it too, the gravity that was pulling them together. He smiled. "Now, what were we talking about? Looking at you makes me forget things."

"Stop it."

"I'm serious." He snapped his fingers. "That's right. We were discussing you leaving med school."

"No, we weren't."

"We almost were," he teased, dimple indenting his cheek. "And how you gave up the life of a highfalutin doctor to become a baker at your mama's café."

She laughed. "Did you really just say 'highfalutin'?"

"I did. Is there something wrong with that term?"

"Only that it's a thousand years old."

"Don't you know what's old is new again?" He smiled and it was contagious. Reece grinned too, her mouth pushing so far up toward her eyes that her face hurt. "If you don't want to talk about it, we don't have to."

"There's really nothing else to say. I like where I am now. I don't know how long it'll last or if I'll decide I want my own place, but for now, while I figure things out, it's good."

He wiped his hands on his napkin and settled it beside the plate. "It's good to have a job where you're busy, one that keeps you moving."

"It is." She frowned. "But you don't work your bar anymore, do you?"

"Not really. I manage it, go in every day and look at the books, but at some point I'm going to sell it."

"Why?"

"I don't want Hadley to see me working at a bar, for that to be how she grows up."

Her heart tightened for how thoughtful Ted was. "You don't think it's moral or something?"

"Let's just say, I wouldn't want my kid to be at my workplace on a Friday or Saturday night. It's a bar. People drink. It can get rowdy." He pointed his finger toward her. "But I'm not ungrateful for all that it's allowed me to do and become—which is a better man than I was before."

She cocked her head, intrigued. "What do you mean?"

"Before I bought that place, I was responsible but still immature. Then when Hadley's mother realized that she was expecting, I buckled down and worked hard to build it into what it is today."

The mention of Hadley's mother made a pang of jealousy shoot through her veins. She forced it aside. It was silly for her to be jealous. Obviously Ted hadn't made Hadley all by himself. There had been a woman involved. But thinking that he'd loved someone else made her feel like someone was shredding her heart with a knife.

"And what's her mother like?"

Ted studied her then, silently weighing something in his mind, or so it seemed. "We were dating when she got pregnant. She'd had a drug problem in the past and had cleaned herself up, but after Hadley was born, she went back to it, and we broke up. It was one of her boyfriends who told me that I needed to get my daughter out of her mama's house because it wasn't safe."

"Oh." She didn't know how to respond. "I'm sorry."

"It's okay. I'd tried getting full custody before then, but it wasn't until I took pictures of the living conditions at her mama's that I was finally granted it." A dark shadow crossed over his jaw before his face shifted and the anger vanished. "But I've got her now and that's all that matters. My mama spends the night a lot so that I can run in the mornings. Then she goes home, and I get Hadley ready for school."

"What grade is she in?"

He lifted one finger. "First, and if the boys don't stop asking to be her boyfriend, it's going to be her last grade because I'm going to have her homeschooled."

She laughed. "She's a pretty little thing. I can see why they like her."

"Too much," he nearly growled before his gaze alighted back on Reece. "Tell me about your made-up boyfriend. What key to your heart does he hold?"

"How did you know he wasn't real?"

"I didn't until you just said it."

She nearly wadded up her napkin and tossed it at him. "I had a very good reason for making him up, thank you very much. Besides, he's not completely fictional. I did have a boyfriend before I went off to med school."

"But let me guess—the grueling schedule and all that studying meant you spent less and less time with him until finally it fizzled out."

"That's right."

A length of silence ignited between them until he finally broke it. "Tell me what you like to do in Sugar Cove."

She shrugged. "I don't know. I work a lot."

"You do, but there's also plenty of time to play. Like, go fishing."

Her eyes widened. "I would love to fish. Last time I was on a boat, we did some treasure hunting with a magnet, but I really wanted to cast a line."

He splayed his hands. "Ask and ye shall receive. It just so happens that I have a boat and rods. All we need is to get you a fishing license."

"I'm in." She smiled and he did, too. Her heart fluttered as she added, "When can we go?"

Ted replied with happiness sparking in his eyes, "Whenever you'd like."

CHAPTER 19

Shelby

Shelby would go to her grave remembering exactly what Batton had said when he broke up with her. *"Your place is here, and I don't want to tie you to something that you don't want."*

"But I want you."

He hadn't said another word, just turned and walked away, ending their relationship and leaving Sugar Cove.

"You okay over there?" her grandmother asked.

She blinked and inhaled sharply, clearing the memory from her head. "Oh yeah, I'm fine."

"Well, it's about time for me to get out of here." She untied her apron and moved to head into the back. "Want me to wait for you? My legs were feeling tired this morning, so I drove."

Shelby's relief was about to arrive anytime. "Nah. You go on ahead. I'll walk home."

She lifted one gray brow. "You sure?"

"I'm sure."

Her grandmother left and a few minutes later Shelby's relief arrived. After working on the previous day's tally and gathering the cash for the bank deposit, she headed out.

She had only just reached the road when a sleek black Tesla pulled into the parking lot. The sun reflected off the windshield, making it impossible to see who was driving the vehicle, see if it was someone she knew.

The car door opened, and her heart stuttered. Batton, wearing slim dark jeans and a white T-shirt, got out, his gaze landing directly onto her.

Fire burned in her veins. What was he doing here? Did he think it was okay for him to come to her store? The place he'd abandoned her to?

Her body screamed at her to cross the road, to keep on her way, but her mind yelled something entirely different, insisting that she give him what for.

Her mind won.

She charged over, hands curled into fists, brows pinched together. "What are you doing here?"

His eyes widened in surprise before narrowing. "Is that the friendly greeting you give all your customers?"

"Very funny. I run into you everywhere I go, even when I'm doing my best to avoid you. But here you are, on my turf."

"I didn't realize this was *West Side Story*."

His mother had a thing for old musicals. Many a Saturday night after supper was spent sitting on the couch with her, his dad and Batton's siblings as they watched musicals that his mother loved.

She smiled at the reference but didn't laugh. "I'm pretty sure that I made myself clear the last time I saw you—I don't want to see you."

Was he trying to torture her with his presence? He'd asked her out, and she'd said no. That should have been the end of it. Batton could help his family and then leave just like he had done in the past.

He shoulders sagged. "Shelby, my mom asked for one of your grandmother's sandwiches."

"She's gone for the day."

"Then I'll come back another time."

He moved to climb back into the Tesla when she said, "No."

"What?"

"No. I don't want you coming here and upending my life." She took a step toward him and stared up into eyes that she'd once loved with all her heart. "You've already done enough damage."

He rocked back onto his heels. "Shelby." The hurt in his voice nearly melted the ice coating her heart. "I only did what I thought was right."

"Right?" Was he kidding? "You broke up with me and left this town. We were supposed to leave together, Batton—you and me. But you abandoned me here."

"To be with your grandmother," he murmured. He tipped his head back and stared into the sky. His shoulders slumped in defeat. "You were worried about leaving her. Do you remember?" He leveled his gaze back on her. "You were concerned about how she'd do without you. You basically told me that you wanted me to break up with you so that you wouldn't have to come with me, so that you wouldn't feel guilty for leaving this town."

Her lower lip quivered. "I never—"

"Yes, you did," he said firmly. "You absolutely told me that. You wanted an excuse to stay, so I gave it to you. But you've blamed me all this time for hurting you, when I was just as hurt, knowing that you wouldn't be able to go. Don't you think it crushed me to do that?"

His voice broke, and so did a sheet of ice that had frosted over her heart. It cracked and fell away. "Why didn't you just tell me?"

"Because you would have denied it." One side of his mouth quirked into the lopsided smile she had loved. "I knew you better than anyone back then. That's exactly what you would have done."

She exhaled a staggering breath, forcing herself to remember. She did recall the guilt that plagued her every time she thought about leaving her grandmother. She couldn't abandon the woman who'd taken care of her for so long.

She dropped her face into her hands. Batton was right. For all these years she'd blamed him for their breakup because he had broken her heart. But when she allowed herself to fall back into the past, she remembered the guilt and worry that she'd been wrapped up in.

She lifted her gaze back to him, expecting him to be angry, but he only smiled and reached out, pushing away a stray strand of hair that the wind had whipped over her mouth.

A shiver rocked her body. How could she have forgotten what being around him was like? How whenever they touched, it was electric, and she could never get enough of him holding her hand, rubbing her back or even squeezing her knee?

"So," she said.

"So," he repeated.

"I guess that I've been blaming you for something that I shouldn't have. You're right, I pushed you away because I was worried about her." It was shameful how she'd blamed him all these years. She felt awful. Shelby shook her head, hoping that the movement would toss the feeling away, but it only intensified. "I'm sorry."

He squeezed her shoulder gently. "There's nothing for you to be sorry for. Your grandmother needed you, and you were right to stay. I'm only sorry that I didn't fight harder."

He would have fought for her? It felt like a giant hand was squeezing every bit of life from her heart. Pain rocked through her body. "It wouldn't have mattered. I couldn't leave then, just like I can't leave now."

One side of his mouth turned up slightly. "What do we do?"

"What do we do?" she repeated as if saying the words would cause them to make more sense.

He rubbed the back of his neck, his gaze dragging from her and scanning left and right, as if waiting for someone to drive down the road. "What I mean is—we can stay like we are, and you can be mean to me whenever we run into each other, or…"

"Or what?" she asked, tilting her head to get a better look at him. Those blue eyes were ringed in gold, and when he looked fully at her, the irises widened, their darkness swallowing the blue.

"Or you can take me up on my offer to go out with me."

"Why?"

"Why not?"

Because wouldn't they just wind up at the same place? Him leaving and her staying? "How will it be different?"

He shifted his weight, which he only did when he was either uncomfortable, thinking or both. "Shelby, I may have left this town, but I never stopped thinking about you. Not once. You were never far from my mind, and yes, I've dated since leaving but no one ever compared to you."

The last bit of ice clinging to her heart cracked off then, falling into the abyss. She licked her lips, and he watched, his gaze flicking to her mouth before landing back on her eyes. "I...I understand. I know what you mean."

Even though she'd had crushes and had dated other men, none of them had ever came close to Batton. Even though she longed for Ted to look at her with something other than sisterly affection, he still wasn't all that she wanted or even needed.

"So then how about it?" he asked, his lips tipping into a smile and his dimple winking at her from his smoothly shaven face. "Would you go out with me?"

Every cell in her body wanted to leap and scream a resounding yes, but her mind took a different turn. "But what about when you leave? Because you and I both know you're not staying here, Batton. You're only here to help your family for a while."

"Shelby, I'm...not so sure that I'm going back."

Her stomach fell. "What?"

"Yeah, there are things going on, and it might be best if I stay."

"What about your job?"

He shrugged. "I can get another one, or I can start my own firm."

"You say it like it's so simple, to leave a life and start another one."

"If there's one thing I've learned," he said as his fingers trailed down the bare flesh of her arm, "it's that there's nothing to be afraid of in life. And if you are afraid, the only thing that'll lead to is more fear."

Batton, staying? There really wasn't any reason for her not to go out with him. He might remain in town, which would mean that she wouldn't get attached and then have to deal with him abandoning her and Sugar Cove again. For once Shelby could let her heart go without worrying about whether or not it would get stomped on.

"Okay," she said quietly.

His eyes sparkled. "Okay, what?"

How adorably annoying. He was going to make her say it. "Okay, Batton, you win. I'll go out with you."

"I don't want you to say it in order to please me. If you're going to do it, I want you to do it because it's what you want."

He was teasing her now. She rolled her eyes even though she wasn't really irritated. "It's what I really want."

"Are you sure?" he asked, rubbing his chin. "Because like I said—"

She reached out and tickled his stomach, causing him to flinch. "It's what I want. Now stop asking me or else I might change my mind."

A slow smile spread across his gorgeous face. "If that's the case, how about we go out tomorrow?"

"Tomorrow?" It was so soon. A knot of worry was building up in her throat, but she swallowed, pushing it back down. There wasn't anything to fear. There was no reason why they couldn't try again, was there? "Tomorrow sounds good. I'd like that."

He started to retreat back to his car. "Pick you up at six?"

"Okay."

"You still living at the same place?"

She pointed toward the house on stilts. "We sure are."

"Then I'll see you then. Tell your grandmother I said hello. I can't wait to see her."

She laughed. "You're more excited to see her than me."

"Absolutely not. But she won my heart a long time ago."

"You're terrible."

"Don't worry. She could never replace you."

With that, she turned and walked toward her house, her heart feeling just a teensy bit lighter.

CHAPTER 20
Ginny

"Tell me, Ginny, is Sugar Cove treating you as well as I suspect it is?"

Ginny sipped the Peanut Butter Bomb milkshake that she'd purchased from the Sugar Shack in Port St. Joe. Her old sorority sister, Molly, walked beside her, sipping her own shake—Oreo. They'd had lunch, brick-oven pizza, at Joe Mama's and had decided to splurge on ice cream to top off their afternoon.

"Sugar Cove is treating me better than you suspect," she confessed, answering her friend's question.

Molly sipped her Oreo shake. "This is heaven."

"I agree."

"So...I hear you've been spending time with Aiden Hassell."

"Oh?" Her brow lifted. "News travels fast, I see."

"He's a pretty big deal around here."

Ginny paused mid-sip. "Is he?"

They stopped to scan the window of a clothing boutique. Molly nodded. "Hm mm. Everyone knows the treasure hunter. He's a local celebrity."

She couldn't help but feel her cheeks burn at the mention of Aiden. "It's not a big deal. We're friends."

"Who've gone out a few times."

"That's right. Molly, I'm not sure if I'm ready for anything."

"I don't blame you there. When I got divorced, it took a long time for me to feel like I was ready to even look at another man."

She sighed. "I can understand that. I've had divorced friends say the same thing. But how do you know about Aiden?"

Molly shrugged before continuing to walk. "Like I said, news travels fast. A lot of women like Aiden, have been interested in him for ages, but he's never reciprocated their feelings. So when you showed up and people started seeing him around with you..." Her lips curled around the straw, and she shot Ginny a knowing look.

"I get it—I quickly became the talk of the town."

"That's exactly right."

She wasn't sure if having that much attention was a good or bad thing. Ginny didn't want to be known as the woman who was dating Aiden. But if that notoriety somehow got her more business, perhaps it wasn't completely bad.

They rounded a corner and nearly bumped into a woman dressed smartly in a light blue dress suit and wearing tall white heels. Her blonde-highlighted brown hair was pulled back into a messy bun, and her face was made up much more than Ginny ever did to her own, with thick eyeliner, dark blush and nude-colored lipstick.

"Ellen," Molly said, greeting the woman, "good to see you."

"Molly, how are you?"

"I'm doing just fine. And yourself?"

Ellen folded her arms, her red-lacquered nails tapping her forearm. "You know, busy. Real estate is booming right now. Everyone wants to move to Florida."

"They do," she agreed. "Have you met my friend, Ginny Rigby?"

Ellen's gaze snapped hard on Ginny, so much so that she nearly choked on a sip of her Peanut Butter Bomb milkshake.

"No, we haven't met yet." Ellen extended her hand. "Pleased to meet you, Ginny."

She took it and smiled. "Nice to meet you."

Ellen stared at her, but it wasn't the sort of look that was simply curious. No, this woman was peering hard, sizing her up. It was unnerving.

"I'd love to stay and chat, but I've to be going," Ellen snapped. "I have a showing."

"Good seeing you," Molly said.

Without another word Ellen stalked off, getting into a convertible Mercedes parked on the street. Her tires squealed as she peeled out of the spot.

"That was…interesting," Ginny said, not wanting to insult Molly, seeing as she was Ellen's friend and all.

"I'm sorry about that."

"What do you mean?"

They continued on before Molly said, "I didn't think she'd be at the office."

She laughed. "What's the big deal?"

They reached Molly's consignment shop just as the door opened and a pretty brunette with a round face and full body emerged.

"Paige, you remember Ginny."

The twentysomething woman smiled at her. "Of course, your sorority sister. Right, Mama?"

"You got it."

"Have y'all had a good time?"

"We had a nice lunch," she told Paige. "You look about the same age as my daughters, Chandler and Reece. You should meet them. I'm sure both my girls could use more girlfriends in town."

Paige nodded eagerly. "That would be great, but Blake takes up a lot of my time."

Molly's face hardened at the mention of her daughter's boyfriend. "Honey, girlfriends are often better than boyfriends."

Her face fell. "I know. But I like spending time with him."

"How long have y'all been dating?" Ginny asked in an attempt to smooth out the tension nearly cracking the air.

"Three years," she answered proudly. "Going on four."

"That's great."

Molly nodded. "Yes, they've been *dating* a long time."

"Mama, not everyone jumps into getting engaged right off the bat."

"Four years isn't right off the bat."

Just then an SUV pulled up and the window rolled down. A man with short dark hair called out from the vehicle. "Hurry up, Paige. We're going to be late. Oh, hello, Molly."

"Blake." Molly's gaze darted from the SUV to Paige. "You have a date?"

"It's a work party," he told her. "At my boss's place, and we're going to be late if Paige doesn't hurry up and get in here."

"Sorry." The young woman ducked her head in apology. "See you later, Mama. Good to see you again, Mrs. Rigby."

Ginny waved. "Bye."

As soon as they were gone, Molly took a long sip from her shake until all that was left was the sound of the straw sucking up air. "That man."

"You don't like him."

Molly sighed and sat on a bench outside of her shop. "He's not right for Paige, doesn't respect her the way that she should be respected."

Ginny joined her on the bench and savored the feel of the warm sun on her face and arms. "Have you talked to her about it?"

"Plenty of times, but she doesn't listen—or care. She says that's just the way he is, that I need to get used to it." Her friend bristled. "I don't want to get used to it. I want her to find someone else. And don't even get me started on the whole they've-been-dating-four-years thing. Actually you don't have to, because I'll go ahead and tell you my thoughts—he's never once suggested marriage."

"Does he want to move in with her?"

Molly gave her a flat look. "Let me clarify—Blake has never talked about moving their relationship to the next level."

"Oh," she replied, cringing. "Doesn't sound like he's interested in doing anything except stringing her along."

"That's what I've tried to tell her, but she won't listen. And worse, I think she feels bad about herself, that she can't get anyone else. But that's just not true. There are plenty of men who come into the shop—dragged in with their mothers or grandmothers—who flirt with Paige, but she doesn't see it."

"Sometimes it's hard to see what's staring us in the face."

Molly nodded. "I know. That's the problem. I just wish that somehow I could show her that there's more fish in the sea than Blake, and that she deserves to be with a man who really loves her, who wants what's best for her and who also worships her."

"She'll find that man."

"I don't know. I'm afraid she's going to waste her whole life on Blake and will only figure out that he doesn't want anything more when she's too old to get those years back."

Ginny nudged her shoulder. "Don't you think you're being a bit dramatic?"

"No. Yes. Maybe. I don't know. I just worry about her, is all."

"Sure you do. Paige is your daughter. You wouldn't be a good mother unless you worried about her. She's lucky to have you."

"Thank you."

Time for a change of subject. If Ginny kept Molly on the topic of Paige, her friend would wind up in a funk over it. "You were going to say something earlier, about that woman Ellen that we ran into."

"Right." She winced. "I'm not sure if you want to know this."

"What could be so bad that I don't want to know?"

When her friend didn't answer, a tingle of worry snaked down her spine. "Okay. It is bad."

"It's not bad, per se, just something that you should be aware of."

"And that is?"

"Ellen is Aiden's ex-wife."

It felt like the world had fallen out from under her feet. He had told her that his wife still lived around here and worked in real estate, but Ginny never suspected that they would run into each other.

"I see," she managed before realizing that her reaction was unfounded. "She's very beautiful and well put together, but you have to be to work in real estate."

"She is beautiful," Molly said in a hesitating voice.

"What is it?"

"It's nothing."

Ginny nudged her shoulder. "Come on. You're holding back. What do you have to tell me?"

"I don't know. I've heard through the grapevine that she's still in love with Aiden."

"Oh." He hadn't mentioned anything like that to her. "But they've been divorced for years."

"Apparently she still holds a torch for him. That's what people say, at least, and you know how tongues wag."

"They do wag."

"They do." They were silent for a moment before Molly gently slapped Ginny's leg. "It's nothing that you have to worry about. If Aiden was interested in her, he would've acted on it a long time ago."

"You're right." She forced herself to smile. "Of course you're right."

Yet Ellen was beautiful. Any man would want her hanging on his arm. But Molly had a point. If Aiden wanted to work things out with his ex-wife, he would've done it a long time ago.

Even though she knew the reality of the situation, she still couldn't stop the pang of worry that burrowed itself into her heart—no matter how hard she tried.

CHAPTER 21
Emma Grace

Diary, I was so ashamed after Papa pulled me away from the fair. I was certain that all was lost. I'd never see Jim again, and he would become nothing more than a memory.

That was until early this morning.

As soon as the sun's first rays show up, Papa always goes to bed. I stay up the first half of the night helping him. But after that, I go to bed so that I can be up and ready for school in the morning.

I had just left the lighthouse when I spotted Jim leaning up against a building, waiting for me.

My heart jumped up into my throat at the sight of him.

But then a wall of shame hit me. I ducked my head, not wanting him to look at me, and started to walk around him, but he reached out and grabbed my hand.

"Stop," I told him.

He dropped my hand as I walked past him, and he hurried to keep up. "You don't want to talk to me?"

"I can't. I'm sorry."

He jumped in front of me then, facing me and walking backward. "I made you something."

I stopped, angry. "Why? Why would you make me anything when my father treated you the way that he did?"

Jim dragged his teeth over his bottom lip. "Because I wanted to, and because I'm not afraid."

I peered into his eyes, looking for any sign of a lie, but didn't see one.

He reached into his pocket and pulled out a small wooden dog. It was about three inches high and had a big, fluffy tail. On one side he'd carved in the most beautiful script, Emma Grace.

He raked his fingers through his hair. "I hope you like it."

"You don't think I'm a dog, do you?" I teased.

His eyes became big as plates. "No, of course not."

I laughed. "I'm only joking. It's beautiful. Thank you."

"It's yours." There was a pause before he said, "Can I walk you to school?"

Heat burned the tops of my cheeks. "Sure."

And so he walked me to school that day and the next. We talked about how exciting it would be to live in a big city full of life, one that's not too far away from the ocean.

Jim told me about the business he wants to have—a big department store, where he sells people what they need at a good price. Then he'll buy a big house and a big car, and—here's the best part, Diary—he wants me to go with him.

But Diary, how can I be with a man my father hates?

* * *

Terrible news. The most awful thing has happened. We were at church on Sunday, and Jim came in with his parents. They haven't been to our church before, and I don't know what made them come that day, but Papa saw Jim's father and something changed in my dad. It was like a light switch had been flipped. He became sullen, with anger simmering inside of him.

Jim's family sat a few rows up from us, but I could see Papa eyeing them. He wasn't even looking at the preacher during the sermon. He just kept his eyes focused on the back of Jim's dad.

I thought things couldn't get any worse, that him being still and quietly angry beside me was enough, but I was wrong.

We were leaving church when it happened. We'd just told the preacher goodbye and were standing outside when Papa told me to wait a moment. Diary, it felt like lightning was shooting through my body I was so nervous.

"Papa, can't we go?" I begged.

His voice was hard, flinty when he answered, "Not yet."

My stomach was so tight that I thought I'd throw up. What was he waiting for? Did he want to yell at Jim? Tell him in front of his parents to leave me alone?

I got my answer as soon as Jim and his parents came out of the church. Papa called out, "Docker."

Jim's father, a lean man with a dark beard and a sun-worn face, searched the crowd until his gaze landed on Papa. His lips pursed as he led his family over to us.

"Will," he said to my father. "It's been a long time."

Papa nodded at him before looking at Jim's mother. "Maureen, you look the same."

That was when Jim's father stepped in front of his wife, blocking her from view. "She made her choice a long time ago."

My father ran his hand down his face. "Your boy's been trying to corrupt my daughter. Seems he's a lot like his father."

Docker's eyes tightened. So did his fists. But he didn't say anything. The whole time this was going on, I'm staring at Jim, wondering what's going to happen, if things will get worse.

Jim kept looking from his dad to mine, and every so often he shot me looks.

Docker said, "Take it back, Will. Take back what you said about my son."

Papa spat on the ground. "I won't. You corrupted Maureen, and your son's trying to do the same thing to Emma Grace. Keep him away from her. I don't want her to end up like the two of you."

"My son's good."

"If he's so good, why's he sneaking my daughter off to fairs without telling her father? Why's he seeing her in secret?"

Docker looked at Jim then, and Jim bowed his head. "I'll deal with my son," he told Papa.

"Keep him away from my daughter," Papa warned again. "The last thing we need is for Emma to become disgraced just like Maureen."

The whole time I had no idea what was going on, Diary. I didn't know why Maureen was so important or how she'd been disgraced.

But those words hit a hard nerve in Jim's dad because the next thing that happened should never occur outside of a church. He pulled back his fist and punched Papa in the nose.

Maureen screamed. Jim grabbed his dad, holding him by the arms. Jim is big, Diary, as tall as his father, if not as broad.

And the worst of it all was that Papa went reeling back, landing on the grass. I reached down to grab him, but he shoved me away.

Docker stepped to my father, towering over him. "Don't you ever say one bad word about my family ever again."

Papa's voice sounded thick, like his nose was stopped up when he answered, "Keep your boy away."

Jim's father gathered his family and they walked away. Papa grabbed a handkerchief from his back pocket and placed it over his nose, which I saw was pushed to one side, broken.

People were staring at us. "Come on," I whispered. He didn't say a thing as we got into the car and headed back.

When we reached the lighthouse, he went into his bedroom and shut the door. I went to my own room and sat for a long time. In my drawer was an old picture of Mother. I pulled it out and looked at the old black-and-white photo, running my fingers over her face.

I miss her, Diary. It was just her and me when Papa went off to the war, and when he came back, she got sick and died. It's just been the two of us for the last five years, and I wish that she was still here. If she was alive, Papa never would have acted like he did at church. He would've just gone on his way. But things were always happier when Mother was living. Ever since her death, there's been a dark shadow over us, over *him*, one that refuses to burn away with the rising sun.

When night came, I went to bed. I had just closed my eyes when a noise made them flutter back open. It came from my window.

My heart leaped into my throat as I opened the window and saw Jim.

"What are you doing here?" I whispered.

"I came to see you."

A slice of moonbeam slashed across his face, and I swear, Diary, that he looked like an angel. My heart was so full from seeing him that I felt as if it might burst.

"I don't know what my father will do if he sees you."

"Then I won't get caught," he said with a smile.

I smiled myself then, before the memory of what had happened at church sank back into my bones. "I'm sorry about today."

"Me too."

"It wasn't your fault." He shrugged and looked away as if ashamed when it was me who should have been ashamed. "What was all of that between them?"

He sighed. "Your father wanted to marry my mother."

It felt like a hammer had been brought down on my head. Never in a million years would I have guessed that. "What?"

Jim swallowed hard, the knot in his throat bobbing. "Then my mother met my dad, and they were caught alone."

My eyes widened. "So that was what Papa meant about corrupting her."

Jim nodded. "They got married a short time after, but from what I understand, your father was going to propose to her. My father beat him to it."

"He loved her," I said, the words barely a whisper. That was why he hated Jim so much. It wasn't because he thought that Jim might steal me away and he'd lose a daughter. It was because he hated Jim's father, pure and simple. He'd wanted to marry a woman who'd loved someone else.

"I'm sorry," I said to him.

"Sorry for what?"

"For all of it, I guess."

"There's nothing for you to be sorry about."

It was then that I knew I loved him, and that we'd never be together. There was no way that my father would ever allow it. He hated Jim's father too much to let me be near his son.

"*Penny for your thoughts,*" he murmured.

"*You'd have to pay me a dollar for them.*"

He tipped his head back and laughed. The sound warmed my body and made me smile.

"*Don't look so sad.*"

"*But I am.*" A tear splashed onto my cheek. "*There's nothing you can do about it.*"

"*I think there's something.*"

"*What's that?*"

"*Marry me.*"

The air was sucked from my lungs. "*You're not serious.*"

"*So serious. More serious than you've seen another person.*"

I studied him, looking for any hint of a smile, but there wasn't one to be found. "*But how will we…?*"

"*Elope,*" he told me. "*We'll get a preacher to marry us. Your father won't be able to say no then. When we come back, he'll have no choice but to accept me as his son. He'll have to get over what happened in the past.*" There was a long pause before he added, "*So will you? Will you marry me?*"

CHAPTER 22
Chandler

"Come sit, Chandler. We haven't seen you in forever. Tell us everything," Evelyn said, patting the cushion beside her.

Hudson's parents had arrived, and their first order of business was to take a boat out to the Gulf and spend the day on the water with Chandler, her mother and sister.

The Wheelers could have insisted on hogging Hudson all to themselves, but they weren't selfish people. Besides, since both families would be joined soon, it made sense that his parents would want to get to know her mother and sister better.

Evelyn looked dazzling in a striped sweater and linen pants. Her short dark hair was windblown and haloed her head. She patted the seat again, and Chandler sat while her mother talked with Hudson's father, Baxter, Bax for short. Hudson and Reece leaned over the boat, peering into the water.

"Have you had a nice trip so far?" she asked Evelyn.

"It's been good seeing Hudson." She smiled toward her son before cocking her head at Chandler. "Your family is just wonderful. I'm impressed with your mother, picking up her life and starting here, and what a great place it is. I'll admit, at first I was nervous about Hudson leaving New York. He's a city boy. But here"—she took a deep inhale

—"it's easy to fall in love with the beach." She nudged her future daughter-in-law's shoulder. "And the people."

"Yes, it is," she agreed. Hudson glanced over and caught her gaze, smiling. She smiled back. "It's a great town."

"And I think Hudson will be happy here," Evelyn said emphatically. "And so will you, if you let yourself."

She frowned. "What do you mean?"

"I think you may know what I mean." She took a deep inhale and stared out at the water. "You've gotten your muse back, which I'm grateful for. Don't get me wrong, but you seem, I don't know, like something isn't right."

"Everything's great." She hoped her smile would convince Evelyn that all was perfect in the world. "Why wouldn't it be?"

"I don't know. Maybe because you've just been through a terrible tragedy, one that rocks, if not topples most families—or people, for that matter. When almost everything you know about someone turns out to be a lie, that's hard to overcome. And if then you're asked to step in a new direction, one that may or may not wind up leading to the same outcome as what nearly destroyed you, that's tough."

Her stomach coiled. How had Evelyn guessed? The look on her face must've said it all because the older woman exhaled heavily.

"You're not the first person I've known to have suffered a severe shock like what your family is still rebuilding from. I've lived in New York a long time, remember? When you have money, it can cause a person to think they're impervious, that they can do whatever they want, smashing people's hearts along the way. I've been lucky with Bax. He holds the same things dear as I do—family, giving back, trying to lead a good life."

"Hudson's great. You've taught him well."

Evelyn studied her closely. "I can't imagine what's going through your mind with the wedding coming up. Have you picked a date yet?"

"No, not yet."

"Mm. Hudson told me you were looking at perhaps a late winter, early spring ceremony."

The truth was that she hadn't picked a date. If she couldn't create his wedding band, how could she pinpoint the perfect time?

But instead of saying all of that, she only replied, "Yes, that's in the works."

"I can help, you know. I mean, I would never want to step on your mother's toes, absolutely not. But if you'd like some insight, someone to bounce ideas off of, I'm here to talk."

"Thank you. I appreciate that."

Evelyn pushed her sunglasses up onto her head. "Of course, if you don't want my help, that's fine, too."

"I'd appreciate whatever you can offer."

"Then might I offer some advice?"

"Of course."

She turned to face Chandler, who did the same. "My advice is to decide who you want to be. Do you want to be someone who worries about what the future holds, a thing that you have no control over. Or do you want to be someone who doesn't, who takes great risks, and with those risks may come great rewards? You've already made so many leaps in life. Don't let what someone else did, no matter how terrible and awful it was, impact the choices you make, especially when it comes to your happiness. I've seen you with my son, and I've seen my son with you. You make each other happy. Let him make you happy, Chandler. That's all he wants to do.

"Besides," she continued, her voice hard, "if you're going to break his heart *again*, it would be better if you did it sooner rather than later."

A lump formed in her throat. Without another word Evelyn patted her shoulder before rising and joining the rest of the party, which had grouped together by the wheel.

His mother had known her fears, had suspected them without Chandler ever saying one word. Evelyn was right. She could either let herself wallow in worry or she could take the bull by the horns.

It was time to decide.

CHAPTER 23
Ginny

"I'm bringing you lunch today," she said into the phone.

Aiden's voice filled with surprise. "To what do I owe the honor of lunch?"

"For fixing my stairs."

"I said that you didn't need to repay me."

"Well," she replied, tucking her left arm under her right one, "what if I told you that I must repay you, that no good deed that is done for me ever goes unrequited?"

He laughed. "Then I suppose that I'd have to take you up on lunch."

"Great. That's what I was hoping. Now. Where's your house?"

"My house is in one place, but I'm not there."

"Oh, mystery man, I see," she teased.

"Not a mystery. I'm in my office."

She frowned. "Office? This is the first I'm hearing of that."

"It's a long story. But you're welcome to bring lunch here—on one condition."

"Oh, you have conditions now?"

"Yes, I do, and that is to join me."

Not a hard decision at all. "Done. Where am I driving to?"

He gave her directions, and a few minutes later she headed out in her sedan, rolling the windows down to let the briny ocean air wind around her hair.

She reached the marina, and just past it was a line of buildings. After parking in the lot, she retrieved the picnic basket and headed inside one office with a sign overhead reading, GULF BOAT ADVENTURES.

Dozens of local businesses offered day fishing and shelling trips for tourists, but she'd had no idea that Aiden owned one.

She walked in and found him behind a desk. When she entered, he rose and came out to greet her. "You're a sight for sore eyes."

Her stomach fluttered at his words. "I'm sorry your eyes are sore."

He smiled. "I'm not."

Their gazes locked for several seconds before she remembered the basket in her hand. She lifted it in offering. "Your lunch."

He took it. "I can't wait to see what you've packed me. Come and sit. I'm sure there are plates and silverware around here somewhere."

While he gathered those, she unpacked the basket, which was filled with fresh fried chicken, a bag of potato chips, fruit salad and pecan pie bites. Those were bite-sized pastry shells filled with pecan pie filling —corn syrup, eggs and brown sugar.

"That looks like heaven," Aiden said, entering the room.

"I can't promise that it'll taste like heaven, but I can only hope."

"If you made it, it'll be amazing. Sit and let me serve you."

She scoffed. "I should be serving you."

"Let me."

When he gently took the box of chicken from her hands, his fingers skimmed her knuckles, sending a jolt of fire down her spine. He plated the food, and she exhaled a shaky breath, leaving her wondering if she'd ever get ahold on her feelings.

She watched as he expertly plated the food and then set it in front of her. "Eat," he commanded.

She giggled. "Are you demanding it?"

"I am."

"And why's that?"

"Because you went to all this trouble, and you deserve to enjoy it as much as I do."

Jack never would have served her like that. He would've expected her to make the food *and* serve it. But Aiden didn't mind doing it at all, and that brought a smile to her face.

"Why're you smiling?"

She shrugged. "Oh, it's nothing. I'm just thinking how much I appreciate you divvying up the meal."

He glanced at her, his blue eyes locking with hers. "It's the least I can do."

Butterflies soared in her stomach, and she looked quickly down at her plate, diverting her attention from his striking eyes and how whenever she looked into them, it felt like she was falling.

"So," she said after he was seated across from her, "what's this business? Are you now charting fishing trips for tourists?"

"Sort of. I'm co-owner, but my partner needed me to buy him out so that he could pay his mom's medical bills."

"Oh no."

"Oh yes, and he kept track of all the paperwork. So I'm trying to figure it out."

"Sounds fun," she joked.

"It's not." He took a bite of chicken and moaned. "Ginny, really, you should've opened a restaurant years ago."

"But then I wouldn't have moved here."

"Good point. Speaking of, isn't it lunchtime at the café?"

"Yes, but I got the girls to cover the second sitting for me. It's our slow day."

"I didn't know you had one of those."

She smiled. "Believe it or not, we do. But back to the story. You bought out his side of the business?"

"Basically." Aiden wiped his fingers on a napkin. "It wasn't easy, and I had to pay him what the business is worth. So now I'm stuck making sure it's successful, which it can be; it just needs a little advertising. There are lots of charter companies, but not one this close to Sugar Cove."

"You could take folks out to St. Vincent Island. Just be sure to warn them about the bees."

He chuckled. "Those were right out of a seventies movie—*Attack of the Killer Bees*."

"I think we dodged a bullet on that one."

It was his turn to chuckle. "You're right."

Their gazes collided again. Ginny didn't look away. Neither did he. She felt the air thicken with tension. There was so much of it that her cheeks warmed.

"Listen," he told her.

"Yes?" she replied, picking at her fruit salad.

"I was wondering if you were free Saturday."

"Saturday? Is something special going on?"

"Let's just say I'd like to repay you for some of the kindness you've shown me."

A laugh bubbled up from her throat. "Kindness that *I've* shown you? You're the one who's given me so much. You repaired those steps without me even having to ask."

"It was nothing."

"It was something to me."

He smiled, which made the corners of his eyes crinkle, making him even more handsome. "After this meal, let's call that even."

"It's not even close," she teased.

"For me it is. But, as I was saying…"

"Yes, as you were saying." She was grinning now, her cheeks hurting because the smile was so big. "Please do continue."

"I'd like to treat you to something special. That's if you're free."

"I'm free."

"Good. Then it's a date."

Her heart stuttered. "A date?"

"Is that okay?"

"Yes."

They'd been out before, so she didn't know why the word *date* had startled her. Maybe it was because they'd gone out to dinner, but Aiden had never formally announced their plans as a date, and that meant she could hide from the truth.

But by actually calling the gathering exactly what it was, a little bit of fear mingled with excitement whirled in her veins.

This was a date. *A date.*

How did she feel about that?

She couldn't imagine going on one with anyone but Aiden. She liked him—a lot, and he liked her.

"Are you sure that's okay?" he prodded.

"Why do you ask?"

"Because you looked scared."

"Oh, I'm not scared." She pressed her left hand to her neck. "Not at all."

He studied her and she wanted to squirm. "Ginny, I don't want to pressure you into anything that you're not ready for."

They'd been to dinner; he'd taken her on his boat. Those had both been dates, she knew that. It was time to get over her worries.

"You're not. I'm excited for whatever surprise you have in store for me." Time to stop talking about dates. "Speaking of surprises, I met your ex-wife the other day."

His eyes widened. Had she said the wrong thing? "How did that go?"

"Fine. She didn't try to scratch my eyes out or anything."

"She wouldn't do that—at least not to your face."

She balked. "What?"

"I'm joking." He covered his hand with hers and her skin tingled. Warmth seeped into her skin, and when he pulled away, she immediately missed his touch. "Ellen is the past."

"I hear she's still in love with you."

He shrugged, glancing toward the front door. "If she is, that's on her. I made it clear a long time ago that our relationship was over. It's been done with a long time." His eyes locked with hers. "There's nothing to worry about with her. I promise."

"Okay."

"However," he added in a voice that made her stomach twist, "she's a bit on the dramatic side."

"What does that mean?"

"It means," he added with a sigh, "that she still hasn't gotten over the divorce, even after all these years."

"Is that something I need to worry about?"

"I don't think so." He clapped his hands. "Now. How about some dessert?"

Ginny grinned as he pulled the bite-sized pecan pies from the basket. "Reece made those just this morning. They should be wonderful."

"I can't wait."

He gave her two, and she stared down at the delicate pastry filled with the corn syrup, molasses and brown sugar medley. Reece had topped each one with roasted pecans. Ginny took a bite and it melted in her mouth.

"These are great," he told her. "Please give my compliments to the chef."

"I certainly will."

As they ate, her mind drifted back to what he had said about Ellen, about how Aiden had said she could be a bit on the dramatic side. He'd also told her not to worry about his ex.

But for some reason Ginny couldn't stop worrying. She just couldn't, because in the back of her mind a thought poked at her. She shouldn't be worried about Ellen, but Ginny had the feeling that she should be. She felt that she should be very worried indeed.

CHAPTER 24
Reece

Reece had been on cloud nine ever since her first date with Ted. It had gone extremely well, so well that she couldn't stop thinking about him. Which was a problem because every time his face or name flitted in her mind, it was joined with a pang of guilt.

She had to tell Shelby the truth. The woman was her best friend in Sugar Cove, and she deserved to know.

But the problem was that every time Reece planned to tell her friend, something always came up—like her guilt, for instance.

"You never told me how your date with Ted was," her mother asked one night when they were having dinner. This was Evelyn and Baxter's last night in town, so Chandler was having dinner with them. This left the other two women to enjoy the evening breeze while listening as the waves slapped against the shore.

"I didn't tell you how it went?" she asked, trying to dodge the question.

Her mother slid a piece of French baguette through the spinach and crab dip that Reece had made for their light supper. "No," she said with a pointed look, "you didn't tell me at all."

"Okay, well, it was..." She cringed.

"It went that well, huh?"

"I wish that I could say otherwise." Things would be so much easier if she could. "But it did go really well. He's already called and asked for another date."

What she didn't mention was that when he called, they spoke for an hour about absolutely nothing and everything at the same time. It felt like she had known him her whole life, which scared and thrilled her.

"Honey, have you told Shelby?"

"And there's the problem." She dragged a slice of baguette through the dip, which was golden brown on top. She took a bite and the zing of the mayonnaise hit her tongue first, followed by the sweet crab meat and the earthy flavor of the spinach. She finished chewing before adding, "No, I haven't told her. I don't know how, and we have another date coming up."

"Usually honesty is the best policy."

"I know." She grimaced. "But this is harder because how am I supposed to break this to Shelby? She likes him so much, and he told me that he doesn't have the same feelings for her. If he did, he would've asked her out a long time ago."

"I can see truth in that. You probably don't want my advice—"

"I do; I want anything you can give me."

"Okay, in my opinion, this is like ripping off a Band-Aid. You can either do it quickly or you can go about it slowly, which is a lot harder because you're in agony the whole time."

"Are you in agony when you take off Band-Aids?" she joked.

Her mother shot her a stern look. "You know what I mean."

"I know. I do." She raked her fingers through her hair. "I just wish it was easier."

She dropped her hands to the table, and her mother reached out, squeezing one. "When you look back on this, you'll see that it was easy, and when Shelby really thinks about it, when she realizes that Ted has never returned her feelings, she'll be happy for you. If she isn't, well then, things might not work out the way that you'd like. But I have a feeling that everything will be okay between y'all."

Reece was tired of talking about her love life, so she expertly changed the subject with, "And how's the diary going?"

Her mother slumped back onto her chair. "Well. Slow because I'm so busy with the café, but overall, very well."

She explained where she was in the story, that Emma Grace and Jim had decided to run off together.

Reece slapped a hand over her mouth before letting it drop. "You're kidding. She's going to up and leave her dad? Run off with this guy? Wasn't that scandalous to do back then? What was this, like seventy years ago?"

"I think so, which would've placed it in the fifties. So yeah, it would've been very inappropriate for her to do such a thing."

"Wow. That's the power of love."

Her mother smiled. "That is the power of love. It helps you make decisions that you otherwise wouldn't have."

"Not sure if that's good or bad."

"It just depends."

Her mother smiled wistfully, and it was obvious that she was thinking about Aiden. Reece liked him. He seemed like a good man, but she still worried. That last thing she wanted was for Mama to get hurt by another man.

"Are we all ready for the Teal Scarf ladies?" her mother asked.

Reece had almost forgotten about the ladies' luncheon they were hosting in a little over a week. "Yes, I think so. The menu's done and the tasting went well, right?

"It did. Mrs. Travis liked all the dishes."

"Then all we need to do is get a little closer and I'll start preparing everything."

"Great, and then we'll need to focus on Thanksgiving."

"Yes. Will it just be us?"

Her mother leaned over and dropped her elbows on the wrought-iron table. "I don't know. Maybe we could invite some other people."

She lifted a brow. "Like Aiden?"

"Maybe. If that's okay with you and your sister."

"It's fine with me, and maybe we can invite Shelby and her grandmother?"

"Of course, and anyone else." She gestured toward the lighthouse. "We have plenty of room inside. We can host fifty people if we want."

She laughed. "Fifty seems like a bit much."

"To me too," her mother said in agreement. "But we can, if you'd want to cook for that many on your day off."

"Let's start with a few and see where we go. Is Hudson coming?"

"He's going to New York, I think."

Reece scraped her teeth over her bottom lip. "Does Chandler seem okay to you?"

"How do you mean?"

"I don't know. She just seems quiet, not as excited as she should be."

Her mother's eyes flashed with worry. "I'm sure she's just got a lot on her mind."

"Maybe."

But she wondered if her sister was still thinking about their father and how her marriage to Hudson could turn out the same way as their parent's. She hoped not, because Hudson was not Jack Rigby.

She was about to say as much when a cell phone rang. Her mother scooped the phone from the table, glanced at it and frowned. She pushed a button on the side, sending the call straight to voice mail.

"Who was that?"

"No one." She shook her head. "Come on. Let's finish this dip before it gets cold."

As Reece dug into the dip, she couldn't help but think that whoever had been on the other line was someone, a secret that her mother didn't want her to know.

CHAPTER 25
Shelby

"Where are we going?"

Batton looked over, his long, dark lashes framing his eyes in a way that made him look ridiculously handsome. Had he always been so handsome?

"If I told you that, then it wouldn't be a surprise."

"I'm not sure if I want you to surprise me."

He chuckled. "We've come too far for you to back down now."

"I'm not backing down," she huffed. "Not from any challenge that you throw at me."

"Point taken. Ah, here we are."

He pulled into the Red Pirate and her jaw dropped. "You're bringing me here?"

"I am."

The local establishment had been around for as long as she could remember. Inside was a family restaurant, but the outside had a mini golf course that was usually inhabited by one or two cats who lived outside.

Batton had brought her here plenty of times in high school, so the fact that he'd return for their first date meant that the place still held meaning for him.

She dragged her gaze from the mini golf course to glance into his eyes. She'd been so hard on him, even had her guard up while they were driving over. But seeing this place made all her defenses crumble.

"I haven't been here in years."

"Me neither."

She grinned. "Which are we doing first—golf or eating?"

"Your pick."

"Golf. I want to work up an appetite."

He laughed, the sound seeping into her bones and making her heart ache for him. "Whatever you'd like."

They got out and bought a round of golf. Two families with elementary-aged children were sprinkled throughout the course, but the first half was open.

Shelby lined up her first shot. "I plan on beating you."

Batton slipped a hand into his pocket and slumped onto one hip. "I wouldn't expect anything less."

"Hole in one. I'm calling it."

"Go for it."

And it was. Her first shot was a hole in one. "Beat that."

He lined up, his strong shoulders and arms making the putter look miniscule in comparison. With one gentle tap of the ball, it rolled down the lane and dropped straight into the cup.

"Looks like you've been practicing."

He plucked the ball from the hole, blew on it and rubbed it on his shirt. "Let's just say when it comes to mini golf, I'm nearly a pro."

A laugh bubbled out of her, but she wasn't about to give up that quickly. For the next eighteen holes, they were neck and neck, Shelby only falling behind when they had reached the last few.

By the time they reached the last two holes, she was down by two points. Batton could easily be overtaken if he'd just...not play so good.

"I'm up." He swung his club and sank the ball in three shots.

She had a chance at winning! Shelby sank her ball in two, which meant she only had to make up one point to tie. If he did poorly on the last hole, she could win.

On the last hole she stepped aside. "You first."

"You sure?"

"I'm sure."

He sank the ball in two strokes. When it was her turn, she noticed sweat slicking her palms. She ran her hands down her shorts and grasped the end of the club.

A hole in one. That was all she needed to tie. She swallowed down a knot in her throat, swung the club back and tapped the ball.

It sailed to the right, hugging the wall, and careened down the slope on its way to the hole. "Come on."

It slipped to the side, skimming the rim, and for a brief second she knew the ball would keep going. But at the last second it circled and sank into the hole.

"Yes!" She jumped. "It's a tie!"

In her excitement at not quite beating Batton but in doing the next best thing, she threw her arms around his neck and hugged him. He stiffened slightly before his fingers curled into her waist and his mouth dropped to her neck. His breath caressed her skin, and it was only then that she realized what she was doing.

Shelby pulled back slightly and tilted her face toward his. Batton straightened and their cheeks grazed as he rose to his full height.

His fingers lightly touched her sides, and her hands rested on his shoulders as if they were about to waltz. Their gazes crashed into one another, and she released a staggering breath.

In that moment she wasn't thinking of all the hurt she had gone through the past years being left by him. She wasn't even thinking about how much her heart had been crushed when Batton left to pursue his dreams. All she knew was that she was lost in his eyes.

Everything stopped. She was supposed to say something, wasn't she? There was a thought in the back of her mind, but it wouldn't quite come.

He spoke first, the right side of his mouth curling into a smile, revealing that dimple. "We tied."

That was what she was going to talk about. She opened her mouth to speak and realized that a huge knot was jamming it up. She swallowed it down, licking her lips in the process. His gaze fell to her mouth, and heat instantly rose on her cheeks.

She released her hands from his shoulders and stepped away. His fingers brushed her waist before falling to his sides. "Yes, we tied. I really wanted to win, but seeing as how you were two strokes ahead and we were down to the last two holes, that was pretty much impossible."

"You still tied. That deserves a treat. Want to grab some food?"

She cocked her brow. "Are you asking me to dinner at the Red Pirate?"

"Unless you'd rather we go somewhere else."

"Nah. This place is fine. You can treat me to a victory dinner."

He grabbed his golf club from the ground, where it had apparently fallen when she'd flung her arms around him. Hers was also on the ground. Shelby hadn't even realized that she'd dropped it.

Before she could get it, Batton plucked it from the Astroturf and smiled at her. His blue eyes were warm, and the softness of his mouth made her want to reach out and touch it to see if it was made of flesh and blood and not putty, like it looked.

But that was silly; she knew how his lips felt, soft and pliable. He walked beside her, his arm brushing hers, and every time it did, it sent little sparks flaring on her skin.

They were seated quickly, and she ordered crab legs and he ordered grilled chicken.

"How's your dad?" she asked.

He sipped a glass of ice water and put it down. "He's getting stronger day by day." His gaze flicked from his glass to her. "My mom asked about you."

Her stomach tightened with sadness. She'd loved his mom so much. When she'd lost Batton, she also lost his family. Sure, she could've kept in touch, but talking to them hurt too much.

"How did you tell her that I'm doing?"

He tsked. "I told her that you found the love of your life and ran off to join the circus as a flying trapeze artist."

She threw a wadded-up straw wrapper at him. "No fair. I didn't get to tell her about how you quit your job to become a pirate and sail the seven seas."

He tossed back his head and laughed. When he righted his face, Batton said, "But that wouldn't have beaten how after you became a trapeze artist, you decided to walk a tightrope between the Empire

State Building and whatever building is closest to it, which was a daring success, I might add."

"So that means I get to tell her that now the British are after you because you sank one of their galleons."

"Those only belonged to the Spanish."

"Same thing."

"Nope. Not at all."

She laughed and it felt like her heart was expanding, like it was sucking on its own canister of helium. She was inflating until she was light enough to float up to the sun, which in this case seemed to be Batton.

"My parents would like to see you."

Her heart stuttered to a stop. "They would?"

"If you want to see them."

He studied her as she considered it. The server appeared out of nowhere and dropped their plates off. They didn't talk as they dived into their food.

The crab legs were tender and sweet, a perfect way to end the evening. "How's your chicken?"

"Good. Want some?"

"No thanks."

"Come on. We used to share food all the time."

"I know, but this is now."

He cut off a chunk of chicken. "I think we should stop comparing now to then. For one thing, it's not doing us any favors." He dropped the chicken that she hadn't asked for on her plate. "For another, we aren't seventeen anymore. We're older, different people, but not so different that my mom doesn't want to see you. Just like she did ten minutes ago when I mentioned it."

Her heart constricted. "This is a lot of pressure."

He ignored her comment. "She wants you over for Sunday dinner."

The crab leg she held nearly slipped from her fingers. "Dinner?"

"Dinner. She won't take no for an answer. You know how my mom is."

"Yes, I do." Dinner with his parents sounded like a lot of pressure.

She hadn't been around them in years, and now they were welcoming her back into the fold as if she and their son were back together.

But they weren't. They'd only played some mini golf and ate some food. They weren't together, and that was what she needed to keep telling herself if she was going to have dinner with his family and not find herself getting too attached to them.

"She'll make a roast," he added, knowing exactly how to tempt her.

"With the yeast rolls?"

He nodded. "With the yeast rolls."

Shelby placed her fists on her hips and said in a mocking voice, "Did your mama say all this so that I'd have no choice but to say yes?"

"I think that is a yes, and to make it even worse, I may have an added surprise for you."

Her stomach dropped because she knew exactly what that surprise was. "You still have the track."

"The one my dad passed down to me?"

"That's the one." She snapped a crab leg in two and pulled out the sweet meat. "We're talking about the electric track, the one with the cars and the guns, and how I used to beat you every time we raced."

He frowned, which created an adorable divot between his brows. She really hated that Batton was so adorable.

"If I remember correctly, I beat you a few times."

"Nope, never happened," she corrected.

"You didn't win every time, Shel."

Her nickname slipping off his lips made her ache for the past. She glanced at the crab legs, composing herself before lifting her chin in defiance. "Oh yes, I did. I won every. Single. Time."

"You're not going to win this time."

"We'll see about that."

"So"—he wadded up his napkin and dropped it atop his plate—"does that mean I can tell my mom to expect you?"

She narrowed her eyes, always ready for a challenge. "Yes, it does."

CHAPTER 26

Ginny

She arrived at Aiden's at exactly seven on the dot. She'd never been to his home before and was shocked as she drove down the driveway.

The house had a steep triangle built into the middle with large windows facing the front. Through those windows she had a clear view of the back of the house, which looked to be completely lined with more windows facing the ocean.

This was a mansion compared to her lighthouse. She parked in front and was about to knock when the door opened.

Aiden stood in the foyer wearing a black apron.

A wave of surprise and nerves flooded her. She brought her hands to her face to stifle her giggle but wound up failing fairly miserably.

"What are you wearing?"

"Tonight, I'm serving you."

She cocked a brow in suspicion. "What?"

He gestured for her to enter. When she did so, he repeated, "I'm serving you tonight. You've served me plenty of times; it's my turn to return the favor."

"Return the favor, huh?" she replied, unable to keep the teasing tone from her voice. "And what about the steps?"

"My gift to you." He closed the door and clapped his hands. "Now. I've got everything set up here."

She followed him, doing her best not to gawk at his home. Ginny couldn't say if she'd ever really been in a bachelor pad before, but when she envisioned a place like that, she imagined black leather couches, a huge television, maybe a neon beer sign.

But this place was nothing like that. Elegant glossy pottery that was clearly art sat atop tables and on pedestals. Potted palms dotted the corners, and several original paintings inspired by the ocean hung on the cream-colored walls.

The windows that she had seen from the outside were just as she had suspected—lining the back wall. They were a good eight feet high and gave the most spectacular view of the sunset. Aiden had his own private beach with one side banked by rocks that the waves crashed against, sending water spraying up over them and pooling below.

"What a view."

"Thank you," he said as he led her to a table butted up to the windows. The living room was open concept that housed the kitchen as well as the *brown* leather couches and television. Sprinkled about the room as well, seated atop small columns like you'd find at a museum, were what looked like relics from shipwrecks.

"Is that a padlock?" she asked, pointing to a piece of metal that was about seven inches long and four inches wide.

He nodded. "It is. It's from the eighteenth century. I found it in the ocean and had it restored."

The iron gleamed under the lights, and though there were a few pockmarks on the metal, overall it looked brand-new. "And it even has the key in it."

He smiled. "That was the best part. It works. Here, I'll show you."

He stepped beside her and took the lock from the column. As he moved past her, he left a trail of brine and pine lingering in the air. How she loved his scent. Aiden turned the key and pulled on the bar that arched atop it, yanking it from the casing.

A huff of surprise blew from her lungs. "That is so neat."

"Here. You can try."

She locked and unlocked the piece before setting it back atop the column. Aiden had stationed himself behind the counter and was busy pulling something from the oven.

"It smells amazing in here."

"Thank you. Please sit."

"Aren't you going to eat with me?"

He shook his head. "This night is all about you."

When had she ever been so pampered by a man? "I can't do that. I'll feel guilty."

"Don't," he said sternly but added a wink. "You don't know it, but you've affected my life in a positive way. The least that I can do is thank you."

"If you insist."

"I do."

She hung her purse over the back of the chair and sat, folded her hands atop the table and waited.

Aiden came out from behind the counter carrying a plate and holding a bottle of wine. "May I pour you a glass?"

"Yes, but not too much. I have to drive."

"Of course."

He filled the glass about one-third of the way and settled a plate before her.

"Are those bacon-wrapped dates?"

He smiled. "Do you like them?"

"I love them. They remind me of Saturday morning breakfasts when the girls were young. That was the one day of the week when we could move slowly, so I'd make pancakes, sausage, eggs, everything they wanted. Then I'd pour warmed syrup over the pancakes, but it would also drip down onto the sausage and when you ate the sausage, it was the best combination of sweet and savory. So yes, I love bacon-wrapped dates."

"Then enjoy."

She frowned. "What are you going to do?"

"Work on the next course."

"There are courses?"

He smirked. "Do I look like I was raised in a barn?"

She laughed. "Plenty of people raised in barns know about three-course meals."

"It was only a figure of speech."

"I know."

She nibbled on a date as he worked. His sleeves were pushed up, revealing strong forearms wrapped in ropes of muscles. Aiden was so much a man—he was strong, liked to work with his hands but also had great business sense. He was just about perfect in every possible way, as Mary Poppins would have said.

But Ginny didn't want to get ahead of herself. She liked him, but she didn't want to be so unrealistic as to think he was perfect. No living person was.

As she stared at him, he glanced up from what he was doing. She jumped, embarrassed for being caught. "How are the dates?"

"Wonderful."

"Are you sure? You looked scared a second ago."

She waved off his concern. "No, I was just deep in thought."

"I'd give more than a penny to know what those thoughts were."

Her gaze skidded away. "Well," she replied, trying to come up with a good answer, "it'll cost you at least a dollar."

He smiled. "I'd gladly pay."

Time to change the subject before she had to admit her thoughts. "What are you making next?"

"That is a surprise."

"Another one? I feel so special."

"You are special."

That time her gaze snapped back to find Aiden staring at her intently. Heat erupted in her belly, fanning out like a fire to her arms and legs. She glanced away quickly, embarrassed.

"It's done."

He brought her a salad made of watercress and filled with hearts of palm. A delicate olive oil–based dressing lightly coated the greens.

"I love watercress."

He leaned against the table. "I had hoped so. It's one of my favorites, too. So's the dressing."

"Did you make it?"

"I did," he said proudly. "If you can believe it, it's an old recipe that Judy Garland shared."

Her brows lifted. "You're joking."

"No. My mom loved it and passed it down to me."

"You are full of surprises tonight."

He leaned his hips against the table and folded his arms. She did her best not to stare at the roped muscles, and thought she did a pretty good job since she stared at her salad instead.

She used her knife to slide some watercress and heart of palm onto her fork and took a bite. The crunch of the delicate watercress mingled with the salty heart of palm and the tangy sweet dressing, was bliss.

She moaned. "Aiden, this is so good. I have to make this at the café. If that's okay, that is."

"I don't know. It's very top secret," he told her with a curve to his mouth.

She laughed. "I would never want to divulge your family's secrets."

"Far be it from me to stop you." They laughed, only to be interrupted by a dinging coming from the kitchen. He pushed off the table. "That would be your main course. Don't worry, you have plenty of time to finish your salad. This needs to cool off."

"Yes, sir."

"So formal," he mused.

"This is a very formal dinner, in case you hadn't noticed. Even down to the white tablecloth."

He winked. "I was hoping you wouldn't notice."

She finished her salad as he prepared whatever surprise he had left. He whisked her plate away and delivered a delicate porcelain plate topped with lightly breaded fish drizzled in a white sauce.

"What is this?" she asked, inhaling the light scent of fish mingled with lemon, and was that...tarragon?

"It's grouper topped with my special sauce."

Her brow curled with intrigue. "Your sauce?"

"That's right. I invented it myself and I like it. However, few others have tried it, so I'm hoping it's up to your standards."

"I'm sure it will be delicious if it's like any of the other dishes I've tried."

"Fingers crossed."

The filet covered most of the plate, and Ginny had already eaten so much that she wasn't sure if she could finish it. "Why don't you sit and join me?"

"Not going to happen."

"Your loss."

"No, it's my gain."

"How so?"

He shrugged. "I like seeing you happy. Watching you smile makes me smile."

Her heart nearly leaped from her chest. What had she done to deserve this goodness in her life? She squeezed his hand.

"I feel the same way." She tasted the fish, and it was just as good as every other dish, if not better. "This is amazing."

"Thank you. Dessert should be ready in a few minutes."

She had eaten most of the fish and was honestly feeling guilty for having him wait on her, so she rose and took the plate to him.

"You didn't have to do that."

She shrugged. "I wanted to. The least I can do to repay you is bring you a plate."

She scanned the kitchen—all stainless steel and top-of-the-line appliances. He even had a double oven.

"You must entertain a lot," she said, nodding toward the feature.

"No, it came with the house." He pressed a hand to his belly. "Even though I may look like a chef, I don't play one in real life."

She giggled and he flashed her a smile that warmed the tops of her ears.

They stared at each other a moment and the air thickened. Her breath caught as he took a step toward her.

That was when the oven timer chimed. The spell broken, Aiden opened the bottom door and pulled out what appeared to be a—

"Chocolate soufflé, madam," he said with a mock bow.

"I'm not eating that all by myself."

"Yes, you are."

"No, I'm not."

He gently placed the chocolate-filled ramekin on a white plate. "Sit and I'll bring it over."

But Ginny was having none of that. She scooped the spoon into the dessert and lightly tasted it. The soufflé was still hot, but not so much that it burned her tongue. The fluffy chocolate dessert melted in her mouth..

"This is amazing. You are so having some of this," she told him.

He frowned, but when she finished her bite, she spooned up more for him. He didn't argue as she slipped the spoon into his mouth.

He moaned. "Oh, that is good."

"That is great," she corrected.

"My turn to feed you." He took the spoon and gently filled it with the dessert before sliding it into her mouth. "Still good?"

"More," she said with a laugh.

He gave her another bite, and she moved to take the spoon from him but when their fingers touched, both of them froze.

She glanced up to see him staring into her eyes. Her breath caught and Aiden slipped closer to her. She couldn't think, couldn't breathe as he dropped his lips to hers and kissed her.

In a blink Ginny was sinking into his arms, savoring the kiss and pushing every thought of Jack from her mind.

This was what she needed, right here, this kiss. When it ended, they each pulled back. He tucked a strand of hair behind her ear, and she smiled.

"You taste like chocolate," she murmured.

He chuckled. "I don't think I've ever kissed a woman who told me that I taste like chocolate."

"There's a first time for everything."

A sparkle twinkled in his eyes. "How about a second time?"

"I'll take that, too."

They kissed again. Ginny didn't know how long they kissed for, but by the time she was leaving for the night—and he insisted on driving her home (she could get her car in the morning)—she was walking on air.

It was only when they said their final good nights that the bubble of happiness burst.

Her phone rang. It was late. Who could it be?

But when she looked down and saw that it was Savannah calling from her old house's landline, her heart froze. What did this woman want? Why did she insist on calling?

Instead of finding out, Ginny pressed a button and muted the call. Nothing was going to ruin her evening, especially not her dead husband's ex-mistress.

CHAPTER 27
Emma Grace

Everything is all set. Jim and I have it planned out, Diary. We're going to leave tomorrow night, right after graduation. I'm going to sneak out while Papa is sleeping. I'll leave a note, of course. But when he wakes up, I'll be gone.

Jim already has a preacher lined up to marry us the next morning out of Tupelo. We'll drive all night until we reach him, marry and start our lives.

It's so crazy, Diary. I'll have my diploma and will be eloping with the man that I love. Jim's parents don't know yet, but he plans to tell them as soon as we marry. That way there won't be anything that anyone can do to change what's done.

We'll be married and that's all there is to it.

But will I be able to wait one more night? Can I suffer through it?

Today is the day. Graduation went great. Papa gave me one of Mama's old brooches for a gift. It's a white cameo on onyx. I'd never seen it before, which means that he'd been saving it for a special occasion.

He had tears in his eyes when he gave it to me. It made me feel awful *for betraying him like I plan to. But I can't think about that right now. I have to pack.*

* * *

I'm packed and ready. I made sure to bring the new brooch and the carving that Jim gave me, the dog with my initials on it. It's a windy day. Jim's out with his father, fishing. It's red snapper season, so the harvest will be good, and they'll make a lot of money. Jim wanted to make sure his dad got every last bit of help that he could offer.

He feels bad leaving his dad, so he talked one of his friends into helping him out until his father finds someone else. I hope his parents aren't too angry at us, at him. But we truly feel that there's no other way to start our lives together except to run off.

I'm sitting at the top of the tower, where I hide you, Diary. Storm clouds are rolling in, and the sky is dark.

I hope Jim and his father come home soon.

* * *

Terrible news. We're in a full-on storm. Rain is lashing the windows, and the waves are crashing against the beach. I haven't heard from Jim, but Papa just got off the phone with the local coast guard. They said that several fishing vessels haven't come in yet, and that Papa needs to make sure the lamp is on now, before the sun sets because the storm has already made the sky so dark.

I can't stop thinking about what the coast guard said, that several fishing vessels haven't come back. They said that they feared the waves could've caused the small boats to capsize. They headed out to search for some of the fisherman, but the storm is so fierce that they had to turn around.

Diary, what if something happens to Jim? I don't know what I'll do. I love him so much.

* * *

It's dark now. The lighthouse lamp is bright, and I've been looking out the windows, trying to see if any boats are approaching the shore, but I haven't seen one. I'm so, so worried about Jim.

I've been pacing back and forth in my room, which is practically impossible since the room is tiny to begin with. But I don't know what else to do with myself.

The wind is howling so loudly that I'm worried it might push the lighthouse over. Papa told me not to worry, that the bricks are strong. But he admitted this storm is a nasty one, and this time of year the Gulf is tormented by strong storms.

He's been getting calls from the coast guard every hour, telling him which boats have come in. All of them have moored except for Jim's. Every single one.

I'm watching out the downstairs window now, waiting, hoping. It's so strange, Diary, how a person's life can change in one minute. One second you think your life is about to begin, and in another you're afraid it'll end before it ever had the chance to take flight.

That's how I feel right now, like I'm suffocating, like Jim is the air I need to survive, and without him there's no food or drink on earth that will nourish me.

Oh, wait. The light washed across the water, and I thought that I saw a boat. My heart is racing while I wait for the light to flood that part of the ocean again.

When it does, I squint as hard as possible, and—it's Jim's boat. It's him and his father! Oh my gosh, they're coming in. They must've lost their sense of direction because they don't normally dock here. But with the storm, they're probably trying to find land no matter where it is.

Now they'll be fine. My heart is soaring. He's safe, and everything will be okay. It's all right if we don't leave tonight. I know they're battered and tired. We can wait. As long as he's safe, that's all I care about.

He'll be here soon. Any time now.

* * *

The lamp went out! Right as Jim and his dad were approaching the shore, the lamp died.

I ran up to the tower, and Papa yelled, "We've got to change it! Hurry!"

He dashed down the stairs to the storage room, where we found the bulb. Then we raced back up and I helped him replace it.

Diary, I've replaced bulbs so many times that I can do it like clockwork, but my hands were shaking so hard that I could barely hold onto the lamp.

By the time we got the lamp on and the light was whirling around, it took me a minute to spot the boat.

And when I did, my heart sank. It was heading directly to the shore.

CHAPTER 28

Ginny

"That's how it ends?" Reece asked.

Ginny placed the diary on the table. "That's it. I don't know how Emma Grace had time to write in it during the storm, but she did."

Chandler nibbled the inside of her mouth. "And then she also had to stash the diary back in the wall."

"That, too." She sighed and sat at the table with them. "It's all still a big mystery about what happened to her. Honestly, I don't feel like we know much more now than we did to begin with."

"Except for the reason why her father hated Jim's dad," Reece pointed out.

"True." She lifted her hands in surrender. "I wish that there was more to it, but that's it."

Chandler pulled the diary to her. "Maybe one of the historical societies will want it."

"Maybe so, honey." She could ask around and see if any were willing to take and preserve the diary. At the very least it was a good snapshot in time, describing what life at the lighthouse had been like seventy years ago. "But until then, we've got a luncheon to get through. Are y'all ready?"

"Aye, aye, captain," Reece said cheerfully with a salute.

She dismissed her silliness with a wave. "Let's make this perfect because I don't think Mrs. Travis will settle for anything less. Oh, here she is now."

A sleek black sedan pulled up, and Sam got out to open the back passenger door. A whirl of excitement rushed through Ginny as she recalled the first time she had met Mrs. Travis and how Aiden had entered the café when the older woman was leaving.

Even though it had been days since their kiss, whenever she focused on it, she could still feel his lips on hers. Honestly she couldn't wait to experience the feeling again. He'd called her the next day, but they'd both been so busy—her with the luncheon and him taking over the charter business—that they hadn't had time to see one another again.

With the way things were looking, they might not get a chance to connect before Thanksgiving, which was quickly approaching.

But her thoughts snapped back to the present when Mrs. Travis entered. She wore a white hat, a coral dress suit fit for a queen, and wound loosely around her neck coiled a teal chiffon scarf.

"Mrs. Travis, good to see you," Ginny said, greeting her with one hand extended.

Mrs. Travis gave the hand a shake and looked the dining room over. "Everything looks beautiful."

Ginny and her daughters had cloaked each table in a white cloth with a teal runner cutting down the middle. Each table would seat four, and the silverware sat atop teal napkins (which she had bought for a steal off the Internet), and water glasses were also set, just waiting to be filled.

"I'm glad you like it," she told the older woman.

Mrs. Travis slowly walked around the dining room, eyeing the tables as if she might find the slightest thing wrong with them, which made Ginny's nerves fray. Instead Mrs. Travis turned and smiled.

"It looks like we're ready for the ladies."

The ladies, as Mrs. Travis had referred to them, began arriving shortly thereafter. There were sixty of them, and each one wore a more dramatic teal scarf than the last. Some were covered in peacocks, another shimmered as if it had been spun with gold, and another was encrusted on the sides with pinky-sized rhinestones.

All in all, the women were very nice and enjoyed the meal. They complimented Ginny and her daughters.

They also kept the three women very busy refilling water and tea, clearing plates and dropping off dessert. By the time the ladies were on the coffee service and Mrs. Travis had risen to speak, Ginny was ready for a nap.

She sat in the kitchen with her daughters, resting, while she listened to Mrs. Travis talk from the dining room.

"Thank you all for coming today and being here with me in Sugar Cove. This town holds special memories for me, and I thought it would be the perfect place for us to have our luncheon."

She went on, talking about the weekend plans she had for the women—touring an art gallery, having tea at the local bed-and-breakfast—all the sorts of things that ladies liked to do.

A few minutes later the speech was finished, and the women were beginning to leave. While Reece and Chandler washed dishes, Ginny cleared the last of the plates and cups off the tables.

"It was a good meal," Mrs. Travis told her. "You did a fine job. And this place..." Her gaze swept around the room. "It was good seeing it again."

Something in her voice nudged at Ginny's heart. "You know it?"

"Somewhat. I passed it every day when I lived here."

"Would you like to see the rest of it?"

Her lips pursed as if she would decline. But a moment later she gave a surprising, "Yes. I would like a tour."

"Well, come on."

She placed the cups she held back on the table and slowly led the older woman past the dining room. "The bedrooms are back here. We only moved in a few months ago, and all we've really done is paint. This lighthouse has good bones."

Mrs. Travis reached out and ran her fingers across some of the exposed bricks. "Yes, it does."

They came to the spiral staircase that led to the tower. "Up there is where the magic used to happen. At the top is the actual working part of the home."

"Yes," the old woman whispered. "So it is." She placed a hand on the wall and closed her eyes.

Ginny reached out, prepared to grab Mrs. Travis if she fell. "Are you feeling all right? Do I need to get your driver?"

Her eyes remained closed. "I'm fine. Just listening."

To the wall? Okay, then. Being from a large city, there was very little that she hadn't heard of when it came to new age spiritual sort of stuff. But she had never experienced someone listening to a wall.

After a long moment Mrs. Travis opened her eyes. Her gaze slowly lifted, and she peered up as if trying to see all the way to the top, which was impossible as the stairway was lined on both sides by brick walls and the steps were made of thickly hewn boards, worn smooth from years of feet going up and down them.

"If I was younger, I would try the trek," she confessed. "But these old legs can't do that anymore. But I wonder"—she looked at Ginny—"what is the view like?"

"It's beautiful. There's ocean as far as the eye can see, and to the left and right are strips of beach and houses. You can also see some of the shops. It's really spectacular, especially at sunset."

"I'm sure it is," she murmured, her eyes wistful. She glanced up the staircase one more time and then slowly turned around. "Thank you for giving me a tour, and thank you for a lovely luncheon."

"It was our pleasure."

Mrs. Travis nodded as if she already knew that. As the two women walked toward the front door, she said, "You'll need to stop by the house this week for your check."

Ginny's stomach dropped. "You won't be paying today? I have the bill ready."

"Oh no. I don't have my checkbook with me. Bring the bill and I'll write the check."

That was a blow. She had expected to be paid on the day of service. But there wasn't any reason to think that the older woman would jilt her, so she nodded. "I'll come Tuesday morning, before the lunch service starts. Is nine thirty too early?"

"Not at all."

"I'll see you then."

When they reached the front door, Sam was waiting to escort Mrs. Travis to the car. As soon as the teal scarf lady was in her car, Ginny grabbed the cups that she'd abandoned on the table and took them to the kitchen to be washed.

Reece glanced up from her spot in front of the sink, where she was rinsing a coffee cup. "Is everyone gone?"

"All gone."

"Let's see the check," she said excitedly.

Ginny sighed. "There was no check."

"What?" Chandler stopped wiping the plate that she held. "What do you mean, there wasn't a check?"

She lifted her hands in both a gesture of surrender and to prove that they were empty. "What I mean is, she didn't write one. She wants me to come see her next week. Then she'll pay."

Her youngest frowned. "You sure do get away with a lot of things when you're older."

"You might be right, honey."

"In the jewelry business you don't get away with anything. If a piece isn't perfect, few will buy it, and if the workmanship is bad, no one will." Chandler lifted a stack of plates and walked them to the cupboard. "But that's just jewelry."

There was something in the slump of her oldest daughter's shoulders that suggested something was wrong. Maybe she was still thinking about what her father had done.

"Reece, I'll finish the dishes. You did so much in preparing the food. Why don't you take off?"

Her eyes flared with surprise. "Are you sure?"

"I'm sure."

Her youngest pulled the apron off her head and hung it on a peg. "Thank you," she said cheerfully before planting a kiss on her cheek.

Ginny laughed at the surprise display of affection. "Why, by the way you're acting, I would think you've got a hot date."

She smiled wide. "I do, and now I can get ready earlier. See y'all later."

"Be sure to let me know when you leave." Her daughter may have been old enough to live her life, but Ginny still worried about her.

"Will do, Mama."

And with that, Reece disappeared from the kitchen.

"Talk about greased lightning," Ginny murmured.

Chandler didn't answer.

"Honey, is there something wrong?" she asked, gently placing the coffee cups in the warm soapy dishwater.

"What would make you ask that?"

"You just seem...unhappy, and I don't want to pry, but..." She very much wanted to pry but needed a good excuse. One came in the leftover Lane Cake sitting atop the counter. "Why don't we have some cake and coffee?"

Her daughter eyed the cake hungrily. "Maybe just a small slice?"

Ginny smiled. "Come and sit. Let's chat and eat."

With that, she plated two slices of cake and headed into the dining room with Chandler not far behind.

CHAPTER 29
Chandler

Chandler sipped the coffee and took a tiny nibble of the Lane Cake. The sponge was moist, and it held a hint of rum that was complimented by the raisins and coconut.

"This is amazing," she said.

"Yes, it is. Reece sure can bake. I'm surprised we haven't seen that until now."

"I know. Her talents were wasted in medical school," she joked, making her mother laugh.

"As much as I'd hate to agree with you, I *agree* with you." They sat in silence for a moment before she went on. "Honey, what's bothering you? Are you still worried about what your father did? Is that still haunting you?"

"It is," she admitted shamefully. "And Evelyn sensed it too when she was here. She told me that I need to make a decision and not hurt her son—*again*."

"She's right."

Chandler smirked. "I know. And what's worse is that I haven't started planning the wedding because of it."

Her mother sucked in a breath. "Honey, you can't lead Hudson on."

"I know that," she snapped. "Sorry. I just...don't know what to do."

"Your heart will tell you. But first and foremost, you need to be honest with Hudson. He has to know. Have you said anything?"

She shook her head, feeling even more shame. "The time hasn't been right."

"It never is when you're the bearer of bad news. But you're an adult, and I didn't raise my daughters to be cowards. You need to tell him the truth," she said sternly. "Today."

"You're right." Tears pricked her eyes. She glanced up at her mother, who was smiling kindly. "I'll tell him tonight."

* * *

"I've been putting off planning the wedding," she admitted to Hudson.

They were strolling along the beach. The sun was sinking fast into the horizon as salt water lapped at their bare feet. Hudson had his khakis rolled up to his calves, and her eyelet sundress slapped her legs as the breeze wound around them before heading inland.

Hudson stopped. The sun was to his back, and it haloed him, making his skin look golden. "Is there a reason why you've been putting it off? I mean, other than the fact that you obviously have to find the perfect venue to marry the perfect man?" he joked.

She smiled. He always made her laugh. "It's nearly impossible to attain that level of perfection on earth."

"It's such a burden." When she didn't respond, he glanced out to the ocean, a shadow falling over his jaw. In that moment his entire mood shifted. "You've been having doubts."

"Yes."

"Do you want to talk about them?"

"Yes."

He started strolling, this time more slowly, his head down, staring at the sand as she talked about her father, about how his betrayal had shaken the very foundation of their family. And how, as much as it made her heart ache to say it, she was worried the same fate would befall her.

He was quiet after she finished, and her heart raced while she waited for Hudson to say something, anything. Sweat slicked her palms, and she wiped them on her sundress.

Hudson caught her hand and held it. "You know I would never do that."

"I know you wouldn't. It's not even a realistic fear. I know that."

"I understand why you're having these doubts. But *Chandler*, I've never, not once given you any reason to think I would do something so heinous. I moved here. For *you*."

Her face heated. "I know that. Like I said, it's not realistic, and I know you love me, and I love you. I know all of that—my heart does. But my mind keeps reminding me of my father's betrayal."

He stopped and shook his head. "I should have known it was too soon. I should've given you more time. But I came all this way"—he gestured inland—"and I thought that would be enough to convince you of how I feel."

She didn't reply because there weren't any words on the tip of her tongue.

He dropped her hand and cupped her face with both of his, tilting her chin up until she was looking at him. "Chan, I love you more than my own life. You are everything to me. *Everything*. But this isn't something that I can convince you of. This is something that you need to work through, because no matter how much I say that I love you and would never, *not ever*, hurt you the way that your father did to your mother, you won't believe me until you're ready, until you've put this out of your heart."

He glanced away, his jaw flexing. It killed her to have to tell him this, to see his pain spreading out before her. Why did she have to feel this way? Why did her stupid heart have to betray her? If she could take back the way she felt and stuff it into a box, lock the box away and never deal with it again, she would. But for now, all Chandler could do was deal with the aftershock of what she'd told him.

After a long moment that felt like eternity spreading out before her, he dragged his gaze back to hers. "How long have you felt this way? Since I proposed?"

"No, a few days after."

He released her cheeks as if her face was on fire and stepped back. He was putting walls up. She instantly recognized the gesture. But what had she expected? Hudson was on the path of marriage. She was on a trajectory that resembled a plane crashing into the side of a mountain.

"I wish you'd told me sooner, hadn't held onto it."

She whispered, "What do we do now?"

He shook his head. He looked away, back to her, away again. When he spoke, his voice sounded as broken as she knew his heart was. "I don't know, Chandler. I don't know. I came all this way for you. I moved here for you. I uprooted my life. *For you.* And now you're telling me that you're afraid I'll turn out like your father? How could you ever think that I'd do something like that? What would ever make you think that? Wait. Don't answer that. I get it. I understand completely why you feel that way. But…it's not rational. Do you see that?"

"I know it's not rational." She wasn't insane, just confused, worried. She did her best to bite back the anger blazing in her gut. "Don't you think I wish that I could get rid of these feelings? That I could stomp on them, and they'd disappear? It's like they're living, breathing beings inside of me, coaxing me to worry about the worst things in the world when I should be focused on the best. I want what you want—to get married, start our lives together. But the level of my dad's betrayal—you can't understand it, Hudson. Your family is perfect."

He scoffed. "Perfect? No family is perfect."

"But yours is. Your dad loves your mom, worships her."

"That doesn't mean they haven't had their share of problems or haven't seen others dealing with situations a lot like yours."

She remembered what his mother had said. There wasn't anything else that she could add other than to whisper, "I'm sorry. Believe me, if I could take back these feelings, I would. The last thing I want to do is hurt you. I love you."

"Is this love?" He threw out his arms. "Sometimes I wonder. Love means working through the hardships, not giving up. But you've already given up. You've created a scenario in your head that doesn't exist and you're leaning into it." He dropped his face into his hands and took a deep breath. When Hudson glanced up, he looked defeated. "I'm going to give you what you want."

Her heart stuttered. "What? I don't want anything. I just wanted to tell you."

"You do want something. You haven't picked a date for the wedding. You haven't shopped for a dress. You haven't done any of that. What you want is for me to end it."

"No, Hudson." Tears pricked her eyes. "That's not what I—"

He lifted his hand to stop her. "Yes, it is. It's exactly what you want. I'm going to give it to you. I'll go home for Thanksgiving, and when I return, I'll pack up and go."

"No."

"It's decided." She started to speak, but he placed a hand over her heart. "If you ask yourself to see the truth, this is what it will tell you."

Tears blurred her vision. This wasn't what she wanted. It was all wrong. *No no no!* It wasn't supposed to end this way. They were supposed to work it out. Hudson would admit that he'd never have a second wife, and she was supposed to feel better. The situation wasn't supposed to take this turn.

"Don't worry. You don't have to see me again."

She closed her eyes and pressed her face to his chest, drinking in his leathery scent. It was her favorite smell in all the world, and she had ruined it. Just because she was so insecure.

He held her for a moment before his arms dropped and he stepped away. She kept her eyes closed while he walked away, up the beach back to his car.

She stood there until she thought she heard the engine start, heard the crashing waves muffle the sound.

She stood there until she was certain that he was gone.

CHAPTER 30
Shelby

Shelby had tried on five different outfits, and none of them were even close to being right. She'd gone through jeans and an off-the-shoulder blouse, a pink sundress, an emerald sheath dress, and even a satiny lavender jumpsuit. But none of them were right. None of them would do when it came to seeing Batton's parents for the first time in ages.

Somehow, even though Sugar Cove was small, Shelby had managed to avoid them like a spy attempting to dodge discovery. This was no small feat in a small town, and she figured if they handed out awards for such a thing, that she would be the front-runner.

After heading back into her closet and pushing aside the clothes again, she finally found a calf-length sapphire-colored skirt loaded with stylish pleats and paired it with a new plum-colored T-shirt that she had bought. The look was perfect—casual but nice. Sunday dinner wasn't something to simply wear torn-up jeans and an old T-shirt to. Stephanie took the dinner seriously, starting on it as soon as they got home from their church's early service. She was home by ten and dinner was on the table by twelve. Plus, it was so fancy that it was never referred to by such a common word as lunch. No, in the South, a nice lunch was called dinner, and dinner could still mean supper.

She put on a light coat of lip gloss and studied herself in the mirror. The T-shirt complimented the skirt perfectly. Her fiery hair hung in loose waves over her shoulders. It was done but not overdone, as if she'd tried too hard. And she kept her makeup to a minimum—mascara, blush and lip gloss. Now was not the time to apply her after-five face.

Butterflies fluttered in her stomach. She took a deep breath. "This is going to be fine. You know these people. Don't worry."

She scraped off gloss from the corner of her mouth with her pinky and headed into the living room, where her grandmother sat snapping green beans. One of the farmers up the road had sold a ton of them to her grandmother. Crops came in late this far South, which was good because that meant they had fresh vegetables and fruit well into fall.

She stopped snapping beans as soon as Shelby entered. "You look nice."

"Thank you," she replied, giving a mock curtsy.

"Stephanie will be impressed by your royal manners."

Shelby rolled her eyes. "That was only for you."

"I'm so blessed," she replied not unkindly. "So, things are going well with Batton?"

"So far." Why was her stomach doing all this flip-flopping? "We'll see."

Her grandmother pulled a string off one side of the beans and dropped it onto a plateful of the castoffs. "Y'all two never should've broken up."

It was impossible to respond to that since Batton had done the breaking up so that Shelby could be with her grandmother and not feel guilty about leaving her.

"And it wouldn't have bothered me at all if you'd gone off with him," she added.

"What's done is done." A knock came from the front door and her stomach dropped. "Time to go."

Though Shelby wanted to charge right on out of the house, Batton stepped inside, caught sight of her grandmother. "Mrs. Thompson, so good to see you. You been doing all right?"

"I've been doing just fine." She smiled widely. "Things are always good in Sugar Cove."

His eyes flashed on Shelby. "Yes, they are."

Pinpricks danced down her spine when he looked at her. It seemed that her body didn't forget how to respond to him. When he touched her, it felt like fire was blazing down her skin, and when their gazes caught, butterflies took flight in her stomach.

It was annoying that her body wouldn't settle down.

"Can I help you snap some beans?" he offered.

What was he doing? They were going to be late.

"You don't have to do that."

"I insist."

And before Shelby knew it, Batton was seated on the couch beside her grandmother, snapping beans. Which made Shelby look ridiculous as the lone person out, so she said, "Scoot over. Let me help."

They snapped beans for a good ten minutes while her grandmother shot questions at Batton—*How're things? How's your mama? I'm so sorry to hear about your dad. He doing okay?*

Frustration built inside Shelby. She didn't know what was going to happen with Batton, and she didn't want to give her grandmother ammunition if he left suddenly, abandoning her again. The last thing she needed was to hear, *He's such a nice boy; whatever happened to him? It's a shame things didn't work out—again.*

That would only put salt on the wounds that would appear if their relationship failed one more time.

Wait. Was it a relationship?

It was certainly something.

Finally Batton brushed his hands and rose. "Looks like we made a good dent in them. If you're still working on them when we return, I'll help you finish."

Her grandmother swatted him. "You don't have to do that to impress me."

"I'm not trying to impress you. I'm impressive enough as it is," he joked in that charming way of his.

She swatted him again, and Shelby swore that heat rose on her grandmother's cheeks. Time to get out of there.

She practically had to pull him out of the house to get them into his car.

When he opened her door, he leaned down and whispered, "You're not jealous because you think I was flirting with Vera, are you?"

"No. Now get in. We're already late."

"We're not. Mama told me that she was running behind."

"Why didn't you say something?"

He shrugged. "Because seeing you frustrated while you snapped beans was too much fun."

She poked him in the chest. "I'm mad at you."

"Well try not to show it when we reach my parents' house," he replied, eyes sparkling with mischief.

It was impossible to be angry with him, but she rolled her eyes and slid onto the seat. He shut the door and got in.

After he'd started the engine and they were on their way, he glanced over. "You look beautiful, by the way."

"I smell like green beans."

He chuckled. "No, you don't." Then he leaned over and sniffed. "Never mind. You do."

If she'd had something in her hand, she would've tossed it at him. "Thanks to you."

"Don't worry. My parents love green beans. It'll make them hungry." She shot him a scorching look and he smiled. "I'm joking. They're excited to see you. All morning my mom's been demanding I go pick you up."

She laughed. "Really?"

"Oh yeah. And Dad's been the same way. I was tempted to call and ask if I could come sooner to pick you up, but changing the time from eleven to nine thirty didn't seem like the right thing to do."

"I was taking a shower then."

"That's what I thought." They drove in silence for a moment until he dropped his hand into the space between them, palm up.

He wanted to hold her hand. They hadn't done that in…years. She shyly slid her palm over his, and Batton squeezed his fingers around hers before kissing the back of her hand.

"Don't be nervous."

Her gaze darted to the window. "I'm not nervous."

"Your palm's sweating."

"It's a condition—it's called sweaty palms. They have commercials on TV all the time for a pill that'll cure it."

"I haven't seen them."

She glanced over and caught him staring at her. A knot swelled in her throat, but she swallowed it down and whispered, "Then you haven't been looking."

"Oh, I've been looking." She laughed and he smiled, which lessened the tension that bunched up her shoulders. He squeezed her hand again. "My parents love you. There's nothing to be nervous about."

"Okay. I'll try not to be nervous."

"What's in the bag?" he asks, glancing down at her feet.

"Oh, it's nothing. Just a new tea towel for your mother. I hope she likes it."

"If it's from you, she'll love it."

Shelby could only hope.

* * *

They arrived at the little bungalow a few minutes later. It was exactly as Shelby remembered it—lemon-yellow boards with white trim and sage-green storm shutters. The front door was painted the same cheery coral as it had been for years.

"Looks the same," she murmured.

"Wait until you see the inside," he said mysteriously.

"What does that mean? Did they renovate?"

He winked. "Just wait."

Stephanie and Chuck answered the door together. Mrs. Deats threw her arms around Shelby's neck and pulled her close. She smelled of vanilla and citrus, two scents that Shelby loved. She'd forgotten how Stephanie always smelled so good.

"We've missed seeing you, darling girl," she told her, pulling away so that Chuck could give her a hug.

Batton's father smelled like an old pipe filled with oak shavings. He gave her a pat on the back, and when she pulled away, Shelby saw how haggard and tired he appeared. He was still recovering from open heart surgery and looked like he needed to be resting instead of entertaining guests.

"Come in, come in," Stephanie ordered.

Batton's mom looked like a mom—her silvery hair was cut into a bob that flipped inside at the shoulders. She wore a turquoise button-down blouse, white capri pants and sandals. She was perfectly round in the middle. Chuck used to affectionately call her filled out, to which Stephanie would pretend to be angry and flick a towel at him.

Shelby remembered those moments fondly. Batton's house had always overflowed with love, and part of her felt like his parents had been her own, which was another reason why she'd been so crushed when he left. Batton didn't just cut himself from her life; he also took Stephanie and Chuck with him.

When she stepped inside, it was like walking into a time capsule. The home looked exactly the same. Somehow Stephanie had brilliantly taken the outside charm of the house and managed to transfer it to the inside.

Exposed birch beams lined the ceiling in the living room. The walls were painted bright white, but one wall was covered in birch paneling, giving the home a comforting, almost nature-like feeling.

The cream-colored couch with overstuffed cushions still sat in the same corner of the open living room. It was accented with sea-green pillows that were just as welcoming as the couch itself.

The entire space was tastefully done and brought back a world of memories—dropping sandy shoes by the door, playing Monopoly on the kitchen table with his parents on rainy days, her grandmother and her coming over to eat big crawfish boils.

Shelby was surprised that she didn't tear up when she walked in, but she was able to tamp down the emotions that threatened to overwhelm her.

"Come in and tell us what you've been up to," Stephanie insisted. "The roast will be done soon."

A roast! Batton's mom made the best roast and potatoes. She always served it with homemade yeast rolls and yep, Shelby smelled the faint trace of yeast mingling with the smell of roasted meat.

They sat in the living room, and she answered every question that his parents peppered her with—*How was she? What had she been up to? How was her grandmother?*

Batton, that lucky dog, sat quietly beside her, not saying a word. Every once in a while her gaze would wander to him, and he'd be sitting there with a small smirk, watching her get asked *all* the questions while he enjoyed not being interrogated.

But it wasn't an interrogation, not really. Talking with Stephanie and Chuck came easily. It was as if no time had passed at all. She learned that Chuck was still recovering from surgery, which was obvious, but that he was slowly regaining his strength.

"I don't know what I'd have done if Batton hadn't come to help," he said.

"He's a good son," Stephanie said proudly.

"He is," Shelby agreed.

Then his mom declared that dinner was ready, and they headed to the table. Shelby insisted on helping, and Stephanie allowed it, giving her dishes to place. She noticed that it took Chuck a little longer to get where he was going, but he wasn't using a walker or any other apparatus to help, so that was good.

When they finished dinner, Batton pulled her from the kitchen, where she was drying dishes. "Come with me."

She shot a worried glance to his mother. "But I'm helping."

"Go." Stephanie waved her off. "We've taken up too much of your time already. You don't have to help. You're our guest."

She begrudgingly finished drying the plate she held and let Batton tug her by the hand into his bedroom. As soon as the door was shut, he kissed her.

Her stomach trembled as if it were filled with a thousand birds that had just scattered. His hands were hot as they held her cheeks, and she stood paralyzed for a moment before letting herself sink and enjoy the feel of his soft lips on hers.

This...*this* was what she wanted. This was what she had been missing for years. She knew that now. Knew that Batton had been the one and only in her life. She had tried to deny it, to convince herself that she didn't want him. But that wasn't the case. The only person she wanted *was* him. And she didn't have to ask to know that he felt the same way.

They parted, and he pressed his forehead to hers, breath coming heavy. She wrapped her fingers around the neck of his T-shirt and relished the feel of his skin against hers, of all the comfort that he brought her.

"Well?" she said.

"Well, what?"

"Aren't we going to play with your race cars?"

He barked a laugh and leaned back against the door. His eyes twinkled with amusement when he said, "You still want to?"

She nudged him playfully with her elbow. "That's what I came over here for."

"It wasn't to see my family and enjoy spending time with me?"

"Nope. Not one bit," she teased.

He laughed and slipped out from against the door. He took her hand and led her to the other side of his bed, where the track and cars were nestled on the floor, just begging to be played with.

She smiled. "You don't disappoint."

A shadow slid over his jaw, and his eyes became troubled. "I don't want to disappoint you, Shelby. Not ever."

Her heart swelled up, and she thought it might break for the look in his eyes.

He took a step toward her and pressed his mouth to her cheek, murmuring the words again. "Never. I never want to disappoint you again."

Her knees wobbled and she felt like she might tip over. Somehow she managed to stay upright and wound her arms around his neck. "I don't want to be disappointed, either."

He squeezed her waist and brushed his lips over her forehead. "If I can help it, it won't happen."

They stood like that a minute before she said, "Are we going to play?"

"Yes." He smiled and stepped back, letting his fingers slide down her arm to take her hand. "Which car do you want to be—the white one or red one?"

Her brow curled as she replied, "The red one, of course."

He chuckled and pulled her down to sit beside him. "Then come on. Let's see who wins."

But Shelby already knew who had won. It was her. She was the winner, and it had nothing to do with cars.

CHAPTER 31

Ginny

Ginny arrived at the home that Mrs. Travis was staying at on time, knowing how the woman liked punctuality. She expected to have a quick visit, which meant doing nothing more than saying hello, taking the check and saying goodbye.

But it appeared that Mrs. Travis had other plans. When Ginny arrived, she found the old woman in the sunroom sitting before a large breakfast spread.

"Please sit," Mrs. Travis said, "have breakfast with me."

She really needed to get back to the café, but she couldn't say no. So she sat across from the older woman and answered the questions that she was peppered with.

"Do you like Sugar Cove?"

"Very much."

"What made you move there?"

Here, she hesitated. "A life change," was the best answer that she could manage. "My family was ready for one, so that's what we did."

Mrs. Travis studied her closely when asking, "Do you like going up into the tower?"

Ginny picked at the fluffy scrambled eggs on her plate. "Honestly, I didn't at first. But I do now. I like it better. I felt very claustrophobic at first. But now it's calmed down."

The old woman nodded in approval. Tired of being asked so many questions that seemed to have come out of nowhere, Ginny said, "Are you all by yourself here?"

"I have Sam, and my assistant is back helping me with day-to-day activities. She's out now," Mrs. Travis explained.

"But what of your things? Did you bring anything from home with you?"

"You mean added luxuries?"

"Yes. You've been here for much longer than a two-week vacation. Where's your family?"

Mrs. Travis smiled wistfully. "When I'm in Sugar Cove, this place is my family. I prefer to come alone."

"Do you bring mementos? Pictures? This house is beautiful, but there don't seem to be many personal touches to it."

In fact, the home felt more like a movie set or a condominium than a place that was lived in. There weren't any family pictures or even knickknacks that suggested the owners' tastes.

Mrs. Travis waved dismissively toward the front of the house. "A few things, but nothing valuable. I prefer to travel light."

The women talked for a few more minutes before Mrs. Travis announced that their meeting was over, and she was ready to hand over payment for the luncheon.

"It was a very nice event," the older woman assured her. "It was good to be back in the lighthouse again."

"When do you leave?"

"Tomorrow morning. I've been here long enough. It's time for me to get back to the city. Now, where did I put that check?"

She searched the table but couldn't find it. A bell sat beside her plate. She rang it, but Sam didn't come.

Mrs. Travis frowned. "He must be busy with something. I'll be right back."

She rose, as did Ginny. "Can I help you?"

"No, no. Meet me in the foyer. I'll return in a moment."

Ginny did as she was asked, taking her time as she made her way back to the front of the house. Though there weren't any knickknacks, beautiful vases and antique porcelain statues dotted the house here and there. Ginny admired them until she reached the door, where a sofa table was butted up against the wall. Sitting atop it was a small wooden statue that looked glaringly out of place.

Curious, she picked it up and turned it around, admiring the lines. Her gaze roved over it, and when it reached the backside, she was so shocked by what she saw that she dropped it, scrambling to catch the statue before it hit the floor.

Her fingers shook as she placed it back atop the table.

"Everything all right?" Mrs. Travis asked, leaning heavily on her cane as she made her way over to Ginny.

"Y-yes. Everything's fine. Thank you." She took the check and smiled. "Tomorrow? That's when you're leaving?"

"Yes. Right after breakfast."

"All right. Have a safe trip."

"Thank you. I would open the door for you, but the cane makes it difficult."

"I understand." Ginny's fingers still trembled as she grabbed the knob and turned it. "I've got it just fine. Travel well."

She had the door open and was about to step through it when Mrs. Travis's voice stopped her. "Thank you again, for everything. Your meal made this trip special."

"You're welcome."

She gave one final nod and stepped out of the house, softly shutting the door behind her. As soon as she was outside, Ginny exhaled a staggering breath before regaining her composure and heading home.

* * *

"Are you sure?" Aiden asked later that afternoon.

Ginny sat on his couch, her feet curled up under her, drinking a cup of hot tea that he had made. No, he hadn't made her chocolate soufflé this time.

But in some ways Ginny almost wished that he had, given that she'd enjoyed their kiss so much. When she thought about it, she could feel his lips on hers, and she wondered when they would share their next kiss.

He sat beside her with a cup of coffee between his hands. The leather couch dipped under his weight, and he sipped his drink before setting it on the table in front of them.

He lifted his brows, silently repeating the question he had asked. Oh, right. He'd asked her something.

"Yes, I'm sure. There's no mistaking it."

He pursed his lips and draped one arm over the back of the couch. "What are you going to do about it?"

She sighed before taking another sip of the herbal tea. "I'm not sure, to be honest. Do you think that I should give it to her?"

"It wouldn't be a bad idea."

"You're right. I'll do that."

She set her tea down, and they stared at one another. They hadn't talked about the kiss. In fact, they'd barely spoken since Saturday. But that was because they were both busy, not because they were avoiding each other.

Right?

"Ginny, I wanted to talk to you about the other night."

Her stomach quivered. Oh no. From the sound of his voice, it seemed like Aiden was about to drop some sort of bomb. Was he going to say that he regretted the kiss? That it wasn't as good as he'd been expecting? That he'd made a mistake?

She felt her face heat as he stared at her. Was there a bed she could dive under? A plant that she could hide behind so that she wouldn't have to deal with his rejection?

But she was a big girl, one who was used to facing life and taking it by the horns. "What did you want to talk about?"

His blue eyes flicked to hers. "When we kissed. I know that you're not ready for anything, and I hope that I didn't overstep any boundaries."

Her stomach dropped before settling. "Boundaries?"

He nodded.

And then she understood. Aiden felt like maybe she'd regretted it.

Her gaze dropped to her lap. "Well, I hope you didn't regret it."

"I don't," he answered quickly. "Do you?"

She shook her head and slowly lifted her gaze until his eyes locked on hers. "Not at all. It was unexpected, but I liked it."

"I know that it's very soon after your husband's death."

She placed her cup of tea on the table near his and slid over on the couch to be closer to him. Aiden opened his arms, and she slipped her hands around his waist as he tugged her close.

"It is soon after Jack's death, but there's something I've learned about that relationship, something that only hindsight could have shown me."

"What's that?" he asked, pressing his chin to the top of her head.

She murmured the words into his chest, using his body as armor to barricade her heart. Because if Aiden rejected her, it would be painful, and she wasn't sure that she was ready for that. But sometimes in life you had to leap and hope that you'd be caught. In this case she hoped Aiden would be the one doing the catching.

"I've learned that I didn't have a relationship with Jack. He gave all the best parts of himself to Savannah and their child. He didn't leave anything for me, and I got used to it. I thought that relationship was the best that I would ever have. Little did I know that there were other fish in the sea, even at my age."

He hugged her tight. "I was worried that the kiss scared you off."

She tipped her head up to stare into those sea-blue eyes. "The last thing it did was scare me. If anything, it made me realize what a drought I was living in. So no, I don't regret it. If anything, I want more."

His eyes widened. "I don't want to give you more than you can take."

"How about I'll tell you when it's too much. And if what you give me is more than I can handle, I'll say so. Then we can pull back."

"You sure?"

His voice was so tender when he asked that her heart ached. How Ginny wished that she'd been given this earlier in her life, that Jack had been more like Aiden. But at the same time, if Jack had been like him, she never would've met Aiden, and she was grateful for their relationship, for how he was teaching her to trust again.

She smiled at him. "I'm sure. I'll say when it's too much."

With that, he dipped his head and kissed her. The kiss was so deep that she forgot about everything except him—all her worries, all her fears. They vanished.

It was only when he pulled back that she came up for air. He pressed her hair from her head and smiled. "Looks like we've got that solved."

She laughed. "We do."

"Now all you have to figure out is what to do about Mrs. Travis."

Ginny scraped her teeth over her bottom lip. "I think I've got that solved, too."

CHAPTER 32
Reece

Being with Ted was like being with someone Reece had known her whole life. He made her laugh, always complimented her, and they never ran out of things to talk about.

When they were out to dinner one night and he looked up at her from across the table and said, "I'd like for you to meet Hadley," her heart nearly fell out onto the floor.

"Meet her? You mean, spend time with her?"

"I mean whatever it is you think I mean."

She rolled her eyes. "That's not the same as actually saying it."

"Okay, then. I'm saying that yes, I'd like for you to join Hadley and myself for an afternoon out. Maybe we can go fishing. Hadley loves fishing, and you do, too."

Her palms were suddenly sweating. This was fairly quickly. She and Ted had only gone out a handful of times. They always had fun and their conversations were full-on discussions about everything from which roast of coffee was the best—lighter or dark—to whether or not aliens really existed, to what was the most important part of life. On that, they both agreed—*family*.

So Reece knew Hadley meant everything to him, which meant that when Ted asked her to spend time with his daughter, this wasn't a decision that he'd come to without carefully considering the consequences.

"I'm a single dad, Reece. You know that I think of Hadley before anyone else. She's the most important person in my life, and you're quickly becoming another important person in my life."

Her cheeks flushed with embarrassment. Suddenly the shrimp on her plate looked way more interesting than his eyes, because she knew that her face must have been on fire.

"You're not looking at me."

"I don't even know what to think right now."

"How about you think," he started in that silky voice of his, "that maybe it might be a good idea for y'all to get to know one another."

Her shoulders slumped. "You're putting a lot of responsibility on me."

"I'm putting a lot of responsibility on both of us," he corrected gently. "I can't bring a woman into my daughter's life unless I'm sure that it's the right thing to do."

She sneaked a glance at him. He stared at her openly, his jaw relaxed, his eyes shining with honesty. "Are you sure it's the right thing?"

"I wouldn't be suggesting it if I wasn't."

And in her heart, if Reece waded through all the worry and knots of anxiety in the way and asked herself if this was the right thing, she knew it was. She knew that Ted was more than a man she would date for a few months and then tire of. She knew that their relationship was bigger, that it was deeper than just surface level.

All she had to do was accept it.

But she also didn't want a ton of pressure on her first time getting to know Hadley. "How about y'all come to Thanksgiving dinner? You, Hadley and your mom? We're cooking up a big feast, and I expect that half the town will be there. I'd like for y'all to come, too."

Ted slowly nodded as if the idea was stewing in his head. "I'd like that, and I'm sure Hadley would enjoy it a lot more than it being just the three of us—and I know for a fact that my mama would rather someone else cook than her."

She laughed. "I bet she would. It's settled."

"It is. We'll come and see how things go. After that, we'll take things from there."

She grinned. "Good. I'll tell Mama to expect—"

Reece was going to say that she would tell her mama to expect three more for Thanksgiving dinner. But she didn't get the words out because as her gaze skimmed the restaurant's dining room, it landed directly on her best friend, Shelby, who was staring at her and Ted.

CHAPTER 33
Shelby

She and Batton had just sat down when Shelby glanced around the dining room of Paddy's Raw Bar on St. George Island. It was a long way to drive for food, but they had trivia night once a week and Shelby loved coming.

But she suddenly forgot about trivia night when her gaze slammed into Reece sitting at a table with Ted. It felt like her heart stopped.

"Everything okay?" Batton asked.

She dragged her gaze from her best friend back to Batton, to really look at him. Ever since Sunday dinner they'd been inseparable. He'd called her every day, and as soon as she was off from work, they were together, doing small things like walking on the beach, running to get ice cream that his mother wanted or playing Monopoly with his family and her grandmother. They even had a cookout last night.

In a few short days Batton had become her world. He had swept in like a tidal wave and had taken over without her even realizing it.

It was as if the years that had come between them had never existed, as if they'd been a bad dream, one where she and Batton had broken up and hadn't spoken. She had lived in a bubble these past few days, and now, seeing Reece, that bubble had burst.

"What is it?" He followed her gaze. "Who's that? Is that Ted?"

Sugar Cove was a small town. Everyone knew everyone else. "Yeah, it's him."

"Is he with a friend of yours?"

"Yes," she murmured.

Batton tapped the edge of the menu on the table. "Shel, you okay?"

She rose. "I'll be right back."

Shelby wasn't sure if she was okay as she rose and made her way to Reece. All her thoughts of how Batton had taken over her life, how he'd become such a large part of it in only a few days, vanished. Now all she could focus on was that her friend was out with the man she had liked.

Shelby reached the table. "Hey, Reece. Hey, Ted."

Ted leaned back in the booth in that relaxed way of his. "Hey, Shelby. How're you doing?"

"I'm good. I'm here with Batton Deats."

His brows lifted. "Good old Batton. He's in town? I had no idea." Ted glanced around her, and a wide smile spread across his face. "I'm gonna go say hello real quick. Be right back."

He winked at Reece before slipping away. As he passed Shelby, he came close enough that she caught a whiff of his scent. Ted smelled musky. It was a good smell, but she'd gotten used to Batton's—fresh soap and cedar.

Reece cleared her throat, and Shelby's gaze dropped to her. "So."

"So." Reece tapped the tabletop nervously. "Batton? Isn't he the guy from Apalach? The one we ran into at the outfitters?"

"The one and only."

"I thought you hated him."

She cringed. "I did. It's a long story, but he's in town because his father had a heart attack, and you know that I'm a sucker and can't be mean to anybody forever. I ran into him a few times, and that's how we wound up"—she gestured behind her to where Batton sat, now across from Ted—"here at Paddy's."

Reece crossed her arms and glanced at her skeptically. "If I remember correctly, you hated him."

"I didn't hate him."

"Yes, you did. You nearly said as much, though I may have been distracted by the fire coming out of your eyes."

Shelby laughed. "Yeah, I was pretty ticked off. But he deserved it."

"Why? What'd he do?" She pushed Ted's plate away. "Sit and tell me everything. Want to order dessert?"

"I just got here."

"Oh, okay. No dessert. But tell me all of it."

As soon as Shelby sat, she spilled every ounce of tea inside of her. She told her friend more about their relationship in high school and why Batton had ended things.

"He did it because of your grandmother?" Reece asked, taking small nibbles from a piece of bread.

"Yeah. I never would have left my grandmother here, and he was right. I couldn't see it at the time, but if I'd gone, I would have felt so guilty." She smoothed her hair with both hands and pulled it over one shoulder. "He thought that he was doing me a favor."

"That's some crazy kind of favor."

"I agree."

The two stared at each other before they burst into laughter. Reece spoke first. "And then you told him that you wouldn't see him *after* you walked an entire grocery store together."

"Yes! I thought I was so suave, getting the upper hand."

She cackled. "But you cracked at the first mention of an electric car race."

"I'm such a cheap date," Shelby joked.

Both women laughed, gazes locked, until the laughter died down and an uncomfortable silence coiled around them. It was Reece who spoke first.

"I'm sorry that I didn't tell you about Ted."

There was a knot in Shelby's throat, one that was lodged high up beside her tonsils. She managed to swallow it down and exhale. "For a long time I liked him. I still do. He's a great guy. But the truth is, if he'd seen me like a girlfriend, he would've asked me out ages ago. But he never has."

"It's not because you aren't beautiful. You're so beautiful," her friend gushed. "If I could take back liking him, I would. But the truth is, he asked me out when we went to his bar that one time."

Her eyes flared in surprise. "I had no idea. Why didn't you say anything?"

"Because you liked him, and your friendship means a lot to me." Reece dropped her head. "The only reason why I ever agreed to dinner was because one day he showed up at the café and I was the only one working. He rolled up his sleeves and helped. Without him the lunch service would have been a disaster."

"That sounds like Ted. He's a good person and a good dad. Have you met Hadley?"

"Once, in passing. He brought her to the café."

"He really liked you from the beginning."

Her friend shrugged as if it wasn't the truth, but Shelby knew that it was. Ted had liked Reece for a long time, and she had been a true friend and hadn't gone out with him until she'd felt like it was the best way to repay him for a service he'd done for her.

If this had been a few weeks ago, before Batton had walked back into her life, Shelby would've been angry. She would've been hurt. But why, she had to ask herself? Would she have been sad simply because Ted didn't feel the same way about her that she felt about him? Would jealousy have caused her to end a friendship?

Shelby hoped that she would have been more mature than that. But right now she did know one thing—she was happy with Batton, so very, very happy.

And she was happy for Reece, too.

She reached over and squeezed her friend's hand. "I'm happy for you and Ted. I really am, and I'm sorry that you didn't feel that you could tell me the truth. From now on, no secrets, even if you think something's going to hurt my feelings. I can handle it. Okay?"

One side of Reece's mouth quirked into a smile. "You got it. No secrets."

Ted was on his way back. Shelby slid out from the booth and made room so that he could retake his spot.

"It was good to see Batton again," he told her. "Says he's going to be staying in town for a while. He's looking for his own place."

Shelby's heart pinged. Batton was going to stay? He was looking for his own place but hadn't told her?

Her gaze skipped across the dining room until it landed on him. He was looking at her and smiling. In that moment her heart ballooned, and Shelby knew that everything, absolutely everything was right in the world.

"Did you know that he was staying?" Reece asked.

"No," she replied absently, "but I do now."

CHAPTER 34
Ginny

Ginny's palms were sweating so badly that every few seconds she had to run them against her linen pants to dry them off. This was a terrible idea. It was the worst. She should back out. It would be easy to turn around and go back the way she had come, to jump in her sedan and drive to the lighthouse.

But she had come this far. It was too late to back out now.

When she pushed the button, the bell inside the house dinged so loudly that it seemed to represent imminent doom. Not good.

She shrugged off the foreboding feeling and waited until the door opened and she was escorted inside. She sat on a bench in the foyer until Mrs. Travis slowly made her way to the room, scowling at what Ginny could only assume was her unannounced presence.

"Was something wrong with the check?" Mrs. Travis asked.

She rose and suddenly her knees were quaking. *I can do this*, she told herself, because a little pep talk never hurt anyone. "No, not at all. I know you're busy, so I don't want to keep you. I have something for you."

Mrs. Travis eyed her skeptically. "Something for me?"

"Yes." She opened her purse and pulled out the diary. "I believe this belongs to you."

Mrs. Travis stared at the book quizzically for half a beat before her face sagged. Did she recognize it? Had Ginny been way off in her suspicion?

The old woman took a slow step forward and extended one withered hand. Her fingers lightly stroked the frayed edge before she traced the gilded frame that bordered the top and sides of the book.

"This...I haven't seen this in years." Her hand trembled and she closed her fist before staring up at Ginny. The old woman's eyes were moist, tears looking to spill any moment. "You found it."

She nodded. "I found it, Emma Grace, and I have a lot of questions."

***

A few minutes later the two women were seated in the parlor, which was accented in the rich colors of lemon yellow and ruby red.

"If I were younger, I would've gone up to the top and found the diary myself," Mrs. Travis explained while the women drank coffee. "But these old legs won't allow me to climb that high anymore."

"You know, you're a legend in these parts. We heard your story not long after we arrived, and it was only by chance that I discovered the diary."

Mrs. Travis brought the cup to her lips and paused. "Have you read it?"

"Every word."

She nodded curtly. "You know my father never would have allowed me to marry Jim."

"Yes, I understand that."

A pause stretched between them before the older woman spoke. "At the time I didn't understand it, and I'm not sure that I do even today. My father had loved Jim's mother so much that he'd never gotten over that she didn't want him. In his mind he made up that she'd been taken advantage of, but the truth was that she loved Jim's father as much as he had loved her. It was a good, true love. I don't know if my father loved my own mother in that way. I would hope so, but one can never be certain. I never spoke to him after the wreck."

There was so much that Ginny wanted to know—all of it, if she was being honest with herself. So she very lightly asked, "What did happen that night? The diary ends with the boat heading toward the shore."

Mrs. Travis stared off Ginny's shoulder. "It was a terrible night. The storm was violent, and you know that Jim's boat hadn't come in."

"And y'all were planning to leave and elope."

"Correct." Her hand shook as she placed the cup atop the saucer and settled the rattling duo atop an end table beside her. "You must forgive me. My nerves are on edge now. I haven't seen that book in seventy years." She inhaled deeply before continuing. "But you were asking about that night. The storm was violent, and I was worried sick about Jim. Finally we saw them. I saw the boat, and that was when the light went out."

"I remember reading that. How horrible."

Her gaze sliced to Ginny. "It was the worst feeling in the world. There was nothing else like it. By the time my father got the light back on, the boat had crashed against the waves."

She brought her trembling hand to her mouth and paused. Ginny didn't want to push her. The older woman would tell the story when she was ready. After a few seconds she started back up.

"I was horrified. My first thought was that Jim was dead, of course. I wasn't thinking, so I ran out to the beach, to the rocks to see if I could help them, or at least recover the bodies. I put on my raincoat and my boots, grabbed a light and headed out.

"My father screamed at me not to go. I told him that I had to, and he said to me that if I went out that door to help that boy, then I shouldn't ever bother coming back."

Ginny winced. How could a father be so cruel to his daughter? How could his heart be so full of anger and hatred that he would say such a thing?

Mrs. Travis continued. "I didn't listen. I went out to the rocks. The night was so black. There was no moon, and there were very few lights on at night back then, not like it is now, where everything is bright. But that's beside the point. I went out and there was Jim, swimming to the shore. His father was beside him, too. The boat was wrecked, but they were alive."

"I helped them both out of the water, but we weren't safe yet, because the wind was lashing and the waves were beating the shore hard.

"Jim's father wanted to go inside, but I told them what my father had said. Right then he understood. He gripped my shoulder and said, 'Then you'll come with us.' And I did." She chewed the inside of her lip a moment as if gathering her next thoughts. "That night I went with Jim and his father, casting off my old life. We made it to their house, and Jim's mother had been so worried that she threw her arms around their necks and cried. Seeing that kind of love in a family made me realize what I'd been missing. It was the sort of love every child, every person should be able to experience. All love should be unconditional, but the world doesn't work like that, does it?"

She shook her head and clasped her hands in her lap. "Jim's father sat us down to figure out what to do with me, I suppose. That was when Jim told him of our plans. That we wanted to marry." Mrs. Travis smiled. "I remember his father smoking his pipe and listening quietly while Jim explained we loved one another. He was silent for a long time before he said that since my father didn't want me to come back and no one knew what had happened to Jim and himself, that maybe the best thing might be to let the two of us have a fresh start."

Ginny didn't understand. "Why?"

"That man understood my father and his jealousy more than I ever did. He knew that if Papa realized that Jim and I had run off together, that he would blame Docker and his wife. My father was so full of spite that he wouldn't have let it go. He would have hounded them until they told him everything. It would have only put gasoline on his fire of already burning anger. Punching Jim's father at church would have only been the beginning of his vengeance."

The dawn of realization hit her. "He told you to fake your deaths."

"You got it." A glimmer of amusement sparkled in her eyes. "Early the next morning Jim's father said his son had been lost at sea and that I had gone into the water to find him and had been lost as well. People searched, but they never found us. Meanwhile Jim and I hid in their house until his parents snuck us out and got us married by a preacher several towns over. And then we left and started our lives."

"What else?" she asked. "What happened after that?"

"We moved to the city, and Jim used all the money he had saved up for years to start a small business. It flourished. We were happy for thirty years until he died from a heart attack. I never really got over it, but I did remarry."

Wow. That was more than a mouthful to chew on. Emma Grace had lived. She wasn't a ghost that haunted the lighthouse. She was an old woman who forged her own path with the man that she loved. But there was still one question left.

"And your father? Did he ever find out the truth?"

Mrs. Travis shook her head sadly. "No, he never did. Years later Jim and I went back to Sugar Cove to visit. I saw him in passing. He'd remarried. Had a new wife and a son. They looked happy, so happy that I didn't want to ruin it by appearing. A few years after that they left Sugar Cove and I never heard about him again. Sometimes I wonder what happened to him and his new family, but they weren't my family, and from what Jim's father told me, he loved his new wife. In some ways that's better medicine to swallow than knowing he didn't love my mother as much as he should have. I hope that he loved his last wife the way that he was supposed to, with all his heart."

Tears pricked Ginny's eyes. "I won't tell anyone that I've met you, or what happened."

Mrs. Travis smiled. "Thank you. I'm an old woman, and the last thing I need is for my life to be upended by the media looking for a story. If people believe I'm a ghost, I'd like to keep things that way."

She lifted her brows. "You *know* what they say about you?"

"I certainly do and find it amusing." Her tone was light, but her gaze dropped to the diary lying beside her. "Thank you for finding this."

"I'm glad that I did, and I'm just glad that I've met you and was able to return the diary to its owner. Now." She settled her cup on the table and smoothed her linen pants with her hands. "I've got a business to run."

Mrs. Travis smiled. "I'll walk you out."

They said their goodbyes at the front door, and as Ginny made her way to the car, her heart felt lighter knowing she'd done the right thing. She might not have been able to tell the world about Mrs. Travis, but she knew the truth and that was enough.

CHAPTER 35
Chandler

Nothing had been the same since Hudson had left. Technically it hadn't been the same since before then, when they'd talked and she'd told him how she felt.

Ever since Chandler had admitted her feelings on the beach, Hudson had been absent in her life, wedging a block of distance between them that made her heart ache so badly that it hurt just to breathe.

This was all her fault, and she knew it.

But there was no turning back.

So when Thanksgiving morning arrived and she was busy preparing dinner alongside Reece and her mother, Chandler couldn't ignore the emptiness in her gut as she made oyster dressing and as she watched her mother carve the turkey.

Everything about it felt wrong.

She wasn't supposed to be alone. She was supposed to be with Hudson, and that feeling worsened the more she stirred, cut and chopped.

It was when she was washing dishes that her mother came over. "What's wrong?"

"Nothing."

"You've been moping all morning. Is it Hudson?"

She dropped her head until her chin rested on her chest. "Yeah, it is. Mama, I've made a terrible mistake. What was I thinking?"

"You were thinking that you needed space and time to figure things out. You may not have known that then, but I suspect you know it now."

A tear streamed down her cheek. "I do know it."

"Go." Her mother turned off the water. "Now. Get out of here."

Where would she go? "What are you talking about?"

"To Hudson. Go to him. Get out of here and spend Thanksgiving with him."

Her gaze skated over the mounds of food prep that still needed to be finished. "But there's so much to do."

"Reece and I will handle it."

Chandler frowned. "Are you sure?"

"Yes, she's sure," her sister called out as she lifted a stack of dishes. "Get out of here."

Her heart swelled with hope. "Only if y'all are sure."

"We're sure," they both shouted.

A laugh bubbled from her throat. She could save this. Chandler could save things with Hudson. But she had to be quick, because the more distance that was put between them, the harder it would be to come back together.

Her mother lightly shoved her toward the back, and Chandler took off to the room she shared with Reece. The first thing she did was call him. His phone went straight to voice mail. She left a message and then called the airline. There was a flight leaving the Panama City Beach airport in an hour and a half. She could make it, but Chandler would have to be quick.

Fast as lightning, she tossed clothes into a suitcase. She wheeled the case into the kitchen, where Reece tossed her a set of keys.

"Take my car."

"You sure?"

Her sister grinned. "Absolutely. Go get that man."

Chandler didn't argue. She grabbed the keys, hugged her family goodbye and set out, determined to win Hudson back.

* * *

As soon as the plane landed, she grabbed an Uber from the East Hampton airport and headed to Sag Harbor, where Hudson's family owned a summer home. It was also the place where they held every big family gathering, including Thanksgiving and Christmas.

Her nerves were on fire as the car made its way toward the house. Would he be happy to see her? Angry?

She'd called him two more times and he hadn't answered. Chandler had even tried Evelyn's phone, but she wasn't answering either, which made sense given how much she had to do to prepare for the meal.

By the time the car dropped her off, her stomach was in knots and sweat was breaking out over her brow, even in the chilly air. The temperature difference between Florida and New York had been a shock, and even though she had brought a thick cardigan to wrap herself in, it wasn't enough to protect her from the frigid air.

She thanked the driver and wheeled the suitcase to the front door. How she wished someone had answered their phone. It would've made this so, so much easier.

But there was no turning back now, and even though she looked like a vagabond appearing with a suitcase on Thanksgiving, it was what it was.

She only prayed that Hudson would talk to her, listen to what she had to say.

The doorbell sounded as loud as thunder when she pushed the button. But she put on her brightest smile and still had it plastered wide when the door swung open, and Evelyn appeared.

"Chandler! Happy Thanksgiving." Evelyn's eyes flared with surprise. "What are you doing here?"

"I'm...um..." Suddenly the words wouldn't come. "I'm...I came to see Hudson."

His mother grimaced. "Well, he's not here. He was. He came last night and stayed, but he left first thing this morning."

Her heart sank. "Do you know where he was going?"

"He said something about going into the city, but he was vague. Oh, honey." She put her arms around her. "I'm sorry. Did you call?"

"I called." Chandler forced herself not to cry. "His phone isn't on."

"I can try to call him."

"No, that's okay." She pulled from the woman's embrace and forced herself to smile. "I just thought that I'd see if he was here."

"I'm sorry. But if he calls, I'll tell him that you came. Listen, why don't you come inside and eat? It's Thanksgiving. You need to be with family."

"Evelyn, who is it?" his father shouted from inside the house.

"It's Chandler."

"Chandler? Well bring her in!"

She stepped back. "No, that's okay. The Uber hasn't left. I'll go."

"But dear—"

She didn't stay. She couldn't. She couldn't bear to go inside and spend Thanksgiving with his family, to be around them when Hudson wasn't there.

Before Evelyn could physically force her into the house, Chandler darted back to the car. Needless to say, the Uber driver was surprised to be returning to the airport.

The journey back was depressing. She watched the scenery go by with a heavy heart. It had been stupid of her to come, to go so far. She was such a fool. Hudson was hurting as much as her. How could she think that she could show up and expect him to be waiting?

She'd pushed him away so much, and he'd given up everything for her. Yet here she was trying to make it up, but her actions had fallen short.

It was too late for them. He didn't want to be with her, and she didn't deserve him.

Chandler had made her bed, and now it was time to lie in it.

She returned to the airline counter and paid for another ticket. There was a flight leaving in two hours. She decided to grab a bite to eat in the meantime.

Her Thanksgiving dinner wouldn't be the traditional cornbread dressing and turkey. A turkey club was the closest thing she was going to get, and she accepted that.

It was after she'd ordered and sat to eat her meal that someone spoke to her.

"Looks like quite the lonely Thanksgiving dinner."

Her stomach tightened as if it were made of piano strings being pulled taut. She didn't dare look up, but she had to.

Chandler's gaze slowly lifted from her plate to look into the face of the man sitting at the table across from her.

Her breath hitched. "Hudson."

His brown eyes were filled with warmth, and one side of his mouth quirked. "Of all the places I expected to run into you, this is the last one."

"I came to see you."

"Me?"

"You."

She slid out from her chair at the same time as he did. His very presence was an oasis in the emotional desert that she'd been lost in these past few weeks.

They didn't stop walking until they were only a foot apart. The air smelled of him—leather and pine. It took all her willpower not to dig her nose into his shoulder and drink up his scent.

He spoke first. "You came to see me?"

"Yes." A knot had balled up in her throat, but she forced it down. "I did. I've...I've been wrong, Hudson. So wrong. I love you so much, and the past doesn't equal the future. It can't. I know that. And for me to project my fears onto you wasn't fair. I came to apologize, and to ask if you'd forgive me."

He tipped his head. "Forgive you? Is that all?"

"It's not all."

"What else?"

There was amusement in his voice, and it made her grin. "Let's see. I also came to see if you'd have me. I won't question your love or even my own anymore. I'm over that. I'm ready to be Mrs. Hudson Wheeler."

"With all your heart?"

"All of it."

"And hope to die?"

"I would gladly stick a needle in my eye for you."

He cringed. "Sounds painful. Maybe don't go that far."

She tipped her head back and laughed. When their gazes collided, he wrapped his arms around her waist and kissed her. She kissed him back, and all the fear that had crusted her heart like ice cracked and fell away.

When they parted, he pressed his forehead to hers. "I was coming back to crash your Thanksgiving."

"That's what I did to your family. I'm pretty sure your mom wanted to send me home with a doggy bag. But I ran out of there before she could."

He barked a laugh. "Tell you what—we can either sit here and have a sad airport Thanksgiving, or we can go back and spend it with my family."

"Mm." She pretended to think about it, but there was no decision to be made. "I pick your family."

He grabbed his suitcase and hers and led Chandler through the airport.

For the first time in a long while Chandler knew that all was right in the world.

CHAPTER 36
Ginny

Ginny's heart couldn't have been any fuller if she'd stuffed it herself. Two long tables lined the dining room of the café, and they were each filled with new friends.

Aiden sat beside her, whispering in her ear as he heaped mashed potatoes onto her plate. Reece sat beside Ted, who'd brought his daughter and mother to the lunch.

From the way that Ted looked at her daughter, it was obvious that he was smitten, maybe even more than that. She hoped to get to know him better in the coming weeks and months.

Shelby had also made an appearance. At first Ginny was worried how things would go over with Ted being there, but she had brought a man named Batton with her. She had also brought her grandmother and Batton's parents. The more, the merrier, Ginny had said as she poured tall glasses of sweet tea for them.

There were more folks than that—regular customers with no family in Sugar Cove. She had welcomed all of them for the meal and was glad to be able to give back to the people who had contributed so much to her happiness.

"Have you heard from Chandler?" Aiden asked.

Just then her phone dinged. "It's her right now."

"What does she say?"

"She's with Hudson and everything's good." She pressed the phone to her chest. "It looks like everyone's having a perfect holiday."

"I definitely am," he told her with a smile that sent a shiver down her spine. "Couldn't be happier."

She nudged him with her shoulder. "Are you sure about that?"

"Oh, I'm sure. Here. Have a bite of pie." Before she could protest, Aiden cut a chunk of pumpkin pie with his fork and fed it to her. "Isn't it good?"

It was. "Mm. Best pie Reece has ever made."

He brushed a strand of hair from her cheek. "This is the best Thanksgiving I've had in a long time."

"Me too."

Her phone rang and she glanced at the number. It was Savannah calling. *Again.* What could that woman possibly want?

Maybe it was because she was so happy. Perhaps it was because it was a holiday and people were supposed to be generous on holidays. Whatever it was, Ginny answered.

"Hello?"

But before Savannah could speak, the door opened with a bang.

Farrah strode in clutching two suitcases. Her eyes were puffy as if she'd been crying, and her gaze searched the room wildly.

Forgetting all about the phone call, Ginny rose and raced to her best friend. "What's wrong? What happened?"

Farrah voice shook. "I've left Brad. It's over."

Ginny's stomach dropped. Well, so much for a perfect holiday. It looked like Thanksgiving was about to be ruined.

Printed in Great Britain
by Amazon